CW01496312

Scarlet Infinity

by

Colin Edge

**Grosvenor House
Publishing Limited**

Colin Edge is hereby identified as author of this
work in accordance with Section 77 of the Copyright, Designs
and Patents Act 1988

The book cover picture is copyright to Inmagine Corp LLC

This book is published by
Grosvenor House Publishing Ltd
28-30 High Street, Guildford, Surrey, GU1 3HY.
www.grosvenorhousepublishing.co.uk

A CIP record for this book
is available from the British Library

ISBN 978-1-906645-70-0

Colin Edge was born in Darlington, England in 1966. He is a graduate of Portsmouth University. He lives and works in London. 'Scarlet Infinity' is his first complete published novel and is part of a trilogy. The follow up 'The Face Man' is currently in production.

For Angela........my infinity!

Contents

CONTENTS

CONTENTS

1

Beach Hut Blues

'There are two kinds of people in this world; those that look when they shouldn't and those that don't look when they should. They walk around Burlington Arcade or Jermyn Street like ants on an anthill, foraging and seething in their own selfish existence looking one way and moving another; the same kind that slow to covet car accidents. Infested with a condition called 'Human', they make up ninety per cent of us. The other group make up a smaller percentage, those that could make a difference. Any difference! But they too need an extra push sometimes, that extra savoir faire.' His thoughts amused him as he took another sip of Absinth from the deep tumbler, its prism crystal cut sides cracked the surf of the Mauritian beach into a hundred kaleidoscope images as just one silent wave rolled ashore. The dark held a stillness, the sunset long since faded. He felt tired, calm and secure. It had been a long day and a long week. He glanced at his watch. It was a little after 3am. The vibrant green glow from its luminous dial drifted into soft focus and he felt his head becoming heavy. A tightness in his wrist from the metal bracelet indicated it was time for slumber. It was time for some well earned down time. He had already reflected on the mission long and hard. His thoughts were now a comfortable calm stream. With lightness and clarity he stood and walked to the welcome embrace of his beach hut bed. Once under the single silk sheet his thoughts drifted. His stubble grazed the pillow and his legs felt like lead. A sudden hoot in the distance and his eyes snapped open; sore against the world. Reaching under the pillow he felt the caress of cold metal. He stood in a single motion and pushed the safety catch with a resonating click! A single red firefly danced a staccato on a nearby veranda wall from the laser aperture. It danced outward kissing the moon with its scarlet infinity. Then the hoot again. This time much closer, much much closer. "Put that down will you!" The red dot found purchase in the cleavage of a familiar female companion.

"Oh Bianco it's you, forgive me. What brings you to my solitary confinement on such a charming evening?"

"We need to speak." She was breathy and jogging lightly. She entered the small stilted hut via the wooden step, breathing heavily now. He couldn't help but glance at the swell of her upper torso. "My dear B what is so important? Our work is done here, and it's 3am." She paused for a moment taking a stifled half breath. "I have something to show you, it's a new development, something we missed." "My dear girl, what is it?" She frantically rummaged through a small black clutch bag. His eyes dropped scanning her curves. Just for a moment he wondered what she would smell and taste like under his single silk sheet.

"This is it!" She held in her hand a small marble sphere with a blue opaque gel inside; slightly smaller than a golf ball.

"My God, where did you get that?" She had a curious smile that started to crack at the side of her lips as she gently swayed her hips like a naughty schoolgirl.

"I did some of my own work. I found it. He left it behind." With eyes transfixed he cupped both hands under hers. "B don't move; breathe if you must!" "Joe stop fooling, what is it?"

"It's a coded Marimba Sphere. I've never actually seen one, and certainly never expected to see one this close up. It was the techies at HQ who told me about them. How long have you had it?"

"About half an hour or so." "Have you handled it much?"

"It was in my palm for about ten minutes after I stole it. I nearly had to secrete it somewhere else to get it out." Before Bianco could finish her sentence, Joseph Sabian vanished skyward over his veranda like a torpedo of freewill. He hit the beach with a thud and a cracking searing pain from his ribs. He turned his weathered chin skyward for a brief moment and felt the hot burst of air pressure as his Mauritian beach hut was torn asunder; as was Bianco. "Poor girl" he groaned.

Bianco was not an agent. He was. He always looked where he was walking, especially when in Jermyn Street and always looked when he should.

2

Coded Marimba Sphere

The "Marimba Sphere" was the latest black market toy of ultimate destruction. Several suicide bombings around the world had employed them. The internal gel was somewhat classified in composition. You couldn't find its make up and chemical formula on the internet, a fact which the Techies at HQ found doubly surprising. Somehow the sphere if handled for a sufficient time would match itself to the hosts body temperature and become coded to the same. Internal reactions would occur with catastrophic consequences. How exactly the spheres worked, no one was quite sure. It was not the sort of thing that found itself into the local patents office. One thing was for sure and well documented, if handled long enough the host could never escape its impending Armageddon. If the host put it down after the period of coded physical alignment they would be part of the secondary explosion after the primary. A number of agents had been lost in the field presumed dead of late trying to infiltrate Ninja terrorist networks. The reconnaissance of the patent type designs for the 'Marimba Sphere' had become the 'raison d'être' of military intelligence organisations globally.

The 'spheres' had first come to notice at a border checkpoint control the previous August, when an eight year old kid approached a group of soldiers. He was playing with what looked like on CCTV playback to be two brightly coloured balls. The resulting explosion was catastrophic; wrecking a small arms hanger and security holding compound. Seventeen dead, including the child; a believed innocent host. HQ had recently received reports of an agent in Budapest finding a case of these things in a semi-finished state. The agent had sent through several high definition JPEG files before being shot at close range by an assassin from the 'Protectors'.

'The Protectors' are an underground ninja terrorist network. Their primary function is believed to be (by those who have got close enough) the manufacture and distribution of the spheres. Places of manufacture had somewhat eluded the authorities, proving a wild and dangerous goose chase for agents across international waters. Tipp-offs rarely led to anywhere other than disused factories, allotments or basements.

The trail of the 'Marimba Spheres' continued.

3

Dead Dinosaur

Joseph Sabian picked himself up from the sand, placing his left hand against the searing pain from a couple of ribs. He spat several grains of sand into orbit and could still feel the crunch of others in his bite. His gait faltered as he took a step forward looking skyward at the vast canvass of stars. 'More stars up there than grains of sand down here!' The pointless thought hammered through his head. He looked toward the beach hut, or at least where it used to be! Splintered fragments of wood and wicker protruded from the stilted platform; like the broken ribs of some long since decayed prehistoric monster. Taking another step he winced from the pain and just for a second Bianco's sweet smiling face projected into his mind, widescreen and in full Technicolor. He whispered her name hopelessly. He walked several more yards, swaying and straining with every seemingly futile movement. Soon he was at the feet of the dead dinosaur. 'No trace of any thing living here!' Of course he knew that would be the case. He knew that from the outset. He noticed a number of blood spattered planks and saw Bianco's small black bag that had been tossed into the nearby gully of a sand dune; its carcass crispy and fried. The sudden smell of freshly cooked bacon invaded his nostrils and he leant forward retching into the sand. Once he had stabilised himself he eagerly retrieved the bag from the gully and forced it open with a sickening ripping noise. The smell hit him again with its subsequent wave of nausea. With that he fell to his knees, cascading forward into the dune, exhausted with pain and emotion. He drifted into the welcome arms of his unconsciousness for a second time. There he lay for a further thirty minutes.

4

Hamus Mehmus

Several miles up the beach in a small hotel apartment overlooking the harbour quay Hamus Mehmus sipped on an ice peppermint tea surveying the armada of luxury yachts tethered below. The Porcupine, Cassandras Crucifix, Naranto and Joannas Javelin were among the dozen or so white streamlined vessels waiting for the stresses of the day. A silent cool breeze kissed Hamus's forehead and he took another sip. A young boy dressed in a cool blue sea- island cotton shirt chased a small dog along a narrow jetty below. He was shouting playfully and waving his arms, "Poncho, Poncho come here, come here now!" Several yards behind a couple in their mid thirties sauntered along hand in hand. She carrying a small light coloured wicker basket and he two fishing rods of differing lengths over his right shoulder. They looked at each other briefly and kissed for a lingering second as they floated along the jetty.

Another peppermint sip and he licked his lips in a slow and deliberately savouring manner. A swirling overhead fan oscillated from inside the cool apartment. Its blades cooled the forming beads of perspiration on his brow as he slipped his light silk dressing gown from his shoulders and discarded it with a single cruel motion into a nearby chair.

The young family boarded the Naranto, the small Jack Russell bounding up at the boy on the deck.

Hamus leant over his bed and placed two plastic tubes, each containing six marble like spheres into the pockets of the black webbing vest that clung to his chest like a second skin. He mumbled under his breath a prayer of salvation and the promise of the fruits of his afterlife. Turning to the blades of the ceiling fan his eyes flickering their whites, he smiled into a grimace. The noise from the fan got louder and louder in his head, whooshing and clipping the air like the rotor blades of some apparition copter in an old Nam movie. He was snapped to reality by the single sound of what reminded him of a marble glancing another in a sock. He thought of how he used to innocently play with marbles as a kid and use an old sock as a convenient carriage for them, and later as a teenager he would use the same as a convenient weapon against disagreeable adversaries (and friends).

The Naranto glided soundlessly from the jetty and toward the mouth of the bay. The translucent water, a mirror to its gleaming white body.

5

Gull Food

The lapping of water at Sabian's feet was both refreshing and alarming. 'How long have I been out?' The heat of the morning sun was slowly crawling up his thighs to his lower back like a blanket of hot writhing ants. The pain in his chest had turned to a comfortable numbness that only spoke louder when he moved in a particular way. The sudden overhead din of seagulls startled him as he turned over onto his back and stared into the big clear blue sky. The ant army was now nibbling at his damaged rib cage and the numbness with the caressing heat was almost a pleasure to hold on to. He turned to his right and saw about a dozen large gulls picking at the bones of the beach hut. His mood darkened for a moment realising it was not the hut they were picking at. A single gull swooped low to where he lay and Sabian instinctively protected his eyes and face with his right hand. He felt something touch his bare chest; a sticky evaporating wetness. He glanced to see a single droplet of blood. He rubbed sand into the stain hurriedly to eradicate the thing and the whole incident from his memory forever. If only he could!

Bianco's black bag was still beside him and he checked the contents, not really thinking about any further possible consequences; the possibility of another Marimba Sphere! He emptied the contents hungrily out onto the sand; too impatient to handle each item. Half a dozen charred remnants lay scattered, amongst them a couple of tampons, an opened chewing gum packet and a Yale type key on a heavy circular brass fob. 'The Palm-Room 203' was deep etched onto it. There was also a memory stick, the name Panasonic leaping out in white bold text on the shiny pink plastic casing. Sabian glanced to the neighbouring sand dune just in time to see two very large gulls having a tug of war with a small piece of red sinewy meat. One of the gulls, the larger of the two squawked and wined like a Hyena as it motioned with a wing like the circling of Count Draculas cloak toward the other gull clipping it around the head and knocking it off balance. The deliberate aggressor took full advantage of the moment, and craning its head back tossed the goblet of Bianco into his throat, swallowing hard, the lump moving like a pressure wave through a fire hydrant hose. Then with the puffing of its chest it was gone skyward and out of site; silent and content.

6

Port Louis

Cafés, bars and trinket gift shops were just starting to open along the quay of Port Louis. The low distant hum of vacuum cleaners and tinkling of crockery sounded the start of another day. Muffled conversations in French could be heard to anyone caring to listen, as menus and hoardings were strategically placed. The signals to the world of available refreshment were becoming starkly evident everywhere. It was market day!

Holly Troupe a twenty seven year old mother of two had just started working at the 'Portico Café' less than a week earlier. She needed the money. Her mother was looking after her two daughters whilst she tried to make a bit of extra cash. This was the first job she had had in a good number of years. She had missed out on a lot in life, including a valuable and benefiting education. This was in the main due to her single determination to bring up her twins. Their father had vanished many years earlier. A one night stand and a broken condom was no way the foundation of a good and fulfilling life, and at just eighteen. This money she needed to go to university and finally pay for her education. Francis Breaget now living in Sicily as a chartered accountant never knew he had a small ready made family half way across the globe.

She looked in the mirror of the small washroom which was just off the kitchen, briefly staring at her pretty but mature face. Her grey blue eyes looked slightly faded of late. She leant closer to the mirror, her breath fogging it whilst a wisp of her brown hair lightly caressed its millpond surface. With her right forefinger she moved and adjusted the contact lens covering her right eye. She blinked frantically a number of times and the soft man made structure settled on the front part of the cylinder it had up until then been swimming around helplessly on. 'Much better' she thought as the lettering on a small packet of Asprin-300mg came sharply into focus on the ledge under the mirror. She adjusted the white polo shirt over her faded blue jeans, the name 'Portico' emblazoned in red italics over the mound of her left breast.

"Holly you done in there?" a thick masculine voice boomed.

"Yeah, just in a mo!" Two minutes later and she was out in the main kitchen area, sliding shiny disposable menus into her back jeans pocket, and tapping her cheap blue biro onto the white note pad. She flicked the pages of the notebook; 'Portico' danced a rhythm of an old film lantern through the pages. The book fell from her clutch and skated to the tiled floor. She bent instinctively to retrieve it. Michael had been watching her and wanted to tell her more than anything in the world how much he was in love with her.

7

How I Miss the Aston

Sabian walked along the beach toward a set of steps chiselled out of the terrain that formed part of the cove that his hut had been situated in. His footsteps were slow but determined. Once at the base of the steps he scanned the fifty that rose before him. How these particular steps had been developed was anyones guess. They looked like the culmination of decades of vegetation trampling and land reclamation. After only ten steps the rise and fall of his ribcage was causing incredible pain. He found by stooping slightly to the injured side to the left he could just about bare it. Once at the top he leant for two minutes against a life ring pole. The buoyancy aid long since gone from its housing with only a dark shadow signifying its once existence remaining. An old shaped Renault 4 sat at the top of the embankment. He found welcome purchase against its nearside battered dented wing. What a mess he thought this particular hire vehicle was. 'How I miss the Aston!" he groaned imagining for a moment that he was playing out a scene from some Fleming novel. After a brief period of taking stock of his situation he fumbled with his watch strap. Holding it limply in his bruised hands it swung like a heavy pendulum in an old grandfather clock, 'to and fro', to and fro' on the end of the thin fabric strap. On the straps security deployment buckle was a small squared device, the size of a standard casino dice but about six times thinner. He slid the device off the strap and pushed a single concealed red plastic button until it clicked! All four door hammers sprung open with a disappointing unsynchronised thud. Opening the front passenger door he half fell into the thing discarding the key fob device into the foot well. He laid motionless, half in and half out of the car. His breathing had become heavy again. He noticed a single wisp of cloud sailing through the perfect blueness above and felt the sticky black plastic of the gear stick knob attacking his right ear lobe and temple. He held the watch out in front of him at arms length then brought it closer and away again as he tried to focus on it. It said it was 308, which he knew was not right, it had stopped about the time of the blast. He noticed that part of the bezel was missing and the crown appeared jammed at a precarious angle. Sabian did not know for sure how long he had drifted in and out of consciousness in his beach paradise.

It was 838 and Holly was serving her first customer at the Portico. His gaze behaviour was erratic and fleetingly regarded Holly as he ordered two ice cold mineral waters. He made her nervous. He was not right. Hamus drank the first glass of water without coming up for air. Two rivers of fluid cascaded each corner of his cruel mouth and onto his khaki olive green shirt under which held a very dark and deadly secret. Holly kept looking back at him as she walked from the tables to the dark recesses of the kitchen. He mumbled spontaneously and began to draw imaginary symbols in the air.

8

Bad News

Dacres, head at HQ was busy in his London office. Joseph Sabian had not called in as promised. Charlotte Mercedes working on secondment to the department and Sabians second out in Mauritius was also off the radar. She had sent a ciphered text a little before 3am that same day, the results of which he was still waiting for. Shortly after 903 there was a knock on his office door. "Come!"

A serious young man in a dark double breasted suit entered the room and silently handed Dacres an envelope marked 'Protected- Highly confidential.' Dacres took it, reluctant to handle the full implication of its possible contents. The young man paused and looked Dacres straight in the eyes. "Leave please, leave now!" With that the young man turned and left the room as quietly and efficiently as he had entered. Dacres opened the envelope and read the contents, the earlier transmission from Mercedes. It included a JPEG image, a little grainy but nonetheless an image identifiable by a man like Dacres and those with his security clearance. "My God!" He gasped.

The secured gates to Downing Street were opened like they knew their place as a black Bentley swung out of

Whitehall and into the small opening, flanked by four police outriders. Blue projected phantoms danced in the Bentleys coachwork and side mirrors as the entourage came to a halt. Three serious looking suited men approached the rear passenger doors. It was to be the worst possible news.

9

The Vulture

The Royal Palm Beach Hotel looked majestic and regal on the edge of Grand Baie. The main drive to its portcullis entrance flanked by palm trees and sprays of sweetly exotic and colourful flowers. Marble graced its high walls; small veins of red flicked through its smooth glacier surfaces. Sabian's car scratched an uneven path through the gates drawing up near two white Roman type columns. The Renault was still moving as the drivers door cracked open, spilling Sabian out onto the dusty terra firma. Through the dust and haze a silhouette moved into view above Sabian blotting out the sunlight; a shimmering vulture in the desert sky high above. A deep voice bellowed down from the vulture. "The investment we have made is now bearing fruit Joseph Sabian!" Joe spluttered and tried to respond, white pressed sand covering his lips and left cheek. "Don't try to speak Sabian; such function you will soon have little use for!"

The sweet intoxicating smell of the flower sprays, musky patcoulioil with a hint of lemon and sandalwood inflamed Sabian's olfactory senses. 'L'instant de Guerlain or Floris flashed through his mind, almost like he had to decide on this minor point in his current predicament.

He was just airing on the side of Guerlain or was it some other cologne when a large black leather steel toe capped boot seemed to graze the stratosphere of his eyeball. It floated weightlessly in its own orbit.

"Who are you?"

"That is, as you know not important!" whispered the Vulture. Sabians breathing had become more laboured and he found himself being sucked into a tunnel of spiralling light as the pain in his ribs melted into the pain he now felt in his skull. Again the welcome blanket of oblivion folded itself around him as the blurry dark bird of prey dived in to feed. When Joe awakened he was in a lavish suite of the Palm. The smell of a cheap pheromone based cologne clung to the air. Joe savoured the smell like a connoisseur would to a finely decanted vintage wine, encoding it for future reference.

"Don't try to move Sabian. I will require a few answers from you before your final expiry from this world." The Vulture had taken human form. Sat in a high backed chair was a large sweating man in his late forties. He had a mop of mousey greasy hair that was thinning on top. He was wearing a light weight black Armani sports jacket two sizes too small. His eyes were fixed on Sabian, the end of a stout snub nosed revolver arrogantly held in his fist. His sausage like fingers gripped and molested the slippery metal. The firing pin was in an open position, and a single swollen finger rested in the circular guard against the trigger. The finger seemed to bulge at its entrance and exit to the black gunmetal ring. The Vulture's mouth moved again, "I take it from your injury and your recently levelled beach accommodation that yourself and the beauty that was Miss Bianco Cellini had a somewhat explosive night together?" Joe did not respond, but waited for death like a hapless traveller waiting for the recoil of a Cobras' venom. The Vulture continued "Mister Sabian are you familiar with the legends surrounding crystal skulls? I pose the question as one of amusement really. I don't really care if you have or if you have not. I'll tell you in any case, because I'm going to kill you in any case!" He sniggered and stroked the grip of the gun with his little finger.

10

The Market

By the second glass of mineral water Hamus Mehmus was getting extremely sticky and hot. Large stained patterns of dampness clung to his underarms that spread their slow and menacing ragged designs along the material of his dense fabric shirt. Spiralling globular orbs of water covered his lower facial hair, each swirling a macabre dance with the sunlight.

The Port market was on a vibrant incline of swelling numbers. Its colourful stall hoardings and banners contrasted the dust grey of the road and building facades nearby. Stall holders opened their wares, rag tag cases and crates. Locally weaved rugs, designer belts and wallets, local food produce, fresh fish, crabs and lobsters still moving on their backs; their legs and tails spiralling a last terminal waltz. Beads and jewellery, amber and anthracite, gleaming and shimmering, casting their gold hues from the sun through minuet rips in the tarpaulins. Characters old and young stumbled around the network of the dusty arena. An old woman threw her head back laughing, the cracks on her face folding and deepening like a dozen weather beaten sails at low tide. Her make-up, high cheek boned rouge gave her the appearance of an insane clown. She took a small bag and emptied it into the middle of her stall still smiling and chatting to those around her. About a dozen cellophane and bubble wrapped wrist watches, Rolex, Cartier and Breitling fell into an unceremonious heap, each priced for less than a snorkel and mask a the local Divers Mart. No warranty papers of course. There was even a limited edition Audemars Piguet not even yet on distribution from their Masterpiece collection, its fake brass case already yellowing and chipping in the repeated bum fights of display and carriage. The smell of fresh and ripe fish with the tang of exotic spices and cooking oils intermingled in the air. The stalls some fifty to sixty in number were separated from the quay by a large and imposing wide dusty road that cut the community in half, leaving all the expensive boutiques on the other. The road was like a fast artery running through, bringing life blood from elsewhere. On the quay a number of cafes had opened and tourists and locals alike gravitated to them, chatting over cappuccinos and ice teas.

Holly was still looking at the suspicious man at table number three in the Portico. He was drawing an elaborate design in mid air with his right index finger. His mouth was moving but no sound came out. Then the odd sound from the back of his throat could be heard, like a poorly synchronised soundtrack on a low budget film. He was oblivious to all and everything around him. He then turned his head slowly and deliberately looking straight at Holly as if he was responding to a sense of being stared at. Holly flinched. His mouth kept moving in its disorganised rumble. He smiled at her, the flesh of his outer gums pulling back over two rows of badly decaying teeth, with one gold tooth flashing front centre, flashing in the sunlight like the dagger of an Arabian assassin. He then spoke in broken French.

"The crusades have never ended by land and by sea and by air!" He smiled again. The market fragrances wafted into the Portico and Holly thought she could taste the stench of his breath in her throat!

1 1

❧❀❧❀❧❀❧❀❧

Strong Mauritian Chilli Rum

The Naranto had sailed steadily on for the last twenty minutes or more. It was well beyond the breakers of the quay. Several luxury yachts glided near the bay and further along the shore line. Bathers along the shore had started to appear in small groups, adjusting large parasols and brightly pastel coloured sun beds. Beach towels were flicked open, sun tan lotion being rubbed and massaged into deep crevices, some golden brown, some lobster red. Drink cans popped and fizzed with levered ring pulls and ice clinked into glass tumblers at the Mephistoe Beach Bar, just open for business.

'Mephistoe Bar' was spray painted in crude blue paint and highlighted in red and green; the words tailing off like a trailblazing asteroid.

"What's your poison?" the thin sprightly barman in shorts enquired. Brunner leant forward tipping his sunglasses off the bridge of his nose and craning slightly to read the array of bottles and pumps. His eyes were drawn to a large demijohn on a homemade wire cradle for ease of pouring. It was three quarters filled with a dark brown liquid. Suspended in the liquid bobbed small black peppercorns and green chillies, floating on their backs all bloated, their goodness and heat long since evacuated into the ocean around them. "You like to try?"

"What is it?"

"Best Mauritian chilli rum my friend." The barman swiftly poured a double shot of it into a small glass with condensation clinging to its sides.

"It's yours for free, on the house as you say, on one condition; you must drink it down in one otherwise you pay! Got it?!"

"Got it!" Brunner took the stiff drink in his right hand staring at it. The barman went on. "My father makes it, it's a local thing. It marinates many months with the chillies. You will like, I'm sure!"

Brunner hesitated.

"Come come, drink drink, hair of the dog as they say. It will put hairs on your chest." Brunner gripped the glass and in a single tossing motion emptied the silky looking contents into the back of his throat and swallowed hard.

The Naranto had her sail at full mast, the wind beating like a rhythmic hammer on its taughtness. Poncho was busy with his head deeply buried in an opened tin of dog food, his small lithe body writhing, his tail beating a frantic rhythm from side to side. Sea spray regularly caught him without interest. Pedelos, yellow and orange battered and skipped their way along the shore line surf as the Naranto ploughed a course sea bound.

It was nine thirty when the blast occurred.

Poncho's head and snout emerged from the tin of Bounet as the dull thunder clap echoed from the direction of the quay. At the very same moment Brunner was coughing, spluttering and finding it hard to catch his breath. His throat was closing as if he had swallowed a dozen razor blades and handful of drawing pins. He heaved again, saliva running from his chin as he stared at the white sand in a stooped position with a single clenched fist in the middle of his chest. The explosion rang in his ears.

Two minutes before at nine twenty eight, Holly Troupe stood frozen as the strangers eyes locked hers in a strange and horrible battle she did not understand. She did not want to. The man stood, his eyes not moving from her. She stepped back instinctively and felt the sudden hard ceramic of the sink buff the small of her back. The man then turned from her as if she no longer mattered and walked slowly and deliberately toward the dusty artery of the main road and busy market. At the same moment in the Palm Hotel Sabian was still staring at his captor with contempt.

"Mister Sabian you have the scent of an assassin, I smelt you as soon as you stepped foot onto this little rock." Sabian grunted and could feel his battered body preparing for fight or flight. "Mister Sabian your government has been very slow. You have presented us with a number of brittle targets. The Marimba Spheres are just the start, a test run if you will. In approximately one minute there will be half a dozen explosions across this little blue marble in some of those brittle targets. The Spheres are just prototypes of bigger and better toys though. Our skulls of doom are twelve times the potency of the Marimba. They use the same principle of the spheres except they look like crystal skulls; carved of pure quartz and each weighing eleven pounds and seven ounces, that's five point nineteen kilograms in new money Mister Sabian. Why skulls you may ask; because of my masters fascination with their legend. Pure amusement only. She likes her toys!"

Holly could not take her eyes off the stranger that had been sat at table number three as he continued walking toward the market and busy road. There was a thunderous terminal screech of brakes followed by the sound of metal, glass, bone and flesh becoming one. The ensuing explosion ripped what was left of the stranger apart as he was tossed skyward like a twisted broken rag doll. He struck the road some ten feet behind the dark blue Honda Civic, its tired tyres smouldering with black sticky tread starting to solidify in small clumps along the tarmac.

12

True English Gentleman

Both Sabian and the Vulture flinched with the sudden dull thud reverberating in the distance. Sabian took advantage of the moment rifling himself free from the bed onto the red Carvern luxury carpet. The Vulture's sausage finger squeezed the trigger; a simple rise in blood pressure would have been enough. The weapon discharged a single bullet. The sausage finger appeared blue and white at its tip as if deprived momentarily of blood and oxygen. The .22 round penetrated the bed, cutting through the quilt, mattress and finally in the dense basket weave it bounced like a captive fallen trapeze artist in a safety net. A dead flattened metal slug!

"What?" Vulture splurted whilst trying to lift his bulk. Sabian under cover of the bed shimmied along the floor several feet through a semi open door that lead to god knows where. Another recoil from the gun and wood with laminate splinters showered the floor from near the door lock. Sabian's breathing felt a whole lot better in the face of the reaper as he lay on his back kicking hard at a small pane of glass leading to a tight veranda. The window popped from its frame and fell in one piece as sudden ferocious pressure was applied from the other side of the door that he was half leaning against. The doors frame shook and shuddered as plaster ruptured from it in several chunks that pelted Sabian's upper arms. Two more shots whistled through the door and over his head. One struck the neighbouring wall; the other shattering a sink. A one inch exit wound gaped in the door. A single bulbous bloodshot eye peered through the wound its black hole constricting as Sabian pulled himself onto the veranda outside. The eye snapped away and in an instant further pressure was being exerted on the French doors next to Sabian. He momentarily sized up the small blue rectangle of the shimmering pool some nine floors below. A tidy shaped brunette in a white thong and bra bathing suite combo looked up in his direction with a double take on him as she fanned out a pink and purple beach towel; draping it over a sun bed. Her eyes blinked rapidly as the Vulture smashed his way through the French doors. Shards of glass ricocheted off the veranda outcrop; falling like tiny droplets of rain; showering the terracotta tiles near a small diving board. The brunette quickly and panicking gathered up her belongings in a clumsy manner; half running, half skipping as she made her way bare footed towards a rear fire exit leading to the reception desk. The Vulture stared at Sabian, his temples pounding and his breathing laboured. His skin had developed a greasy sweaty patina. Limply he held the revolver in his right fist as a fly buzzed an arc around his head; following up with a reconnaissance move toward his open foul smelling mouth. His cologne was obviously attracting some of the locals. He waved his gun fist at the irritant. Sabian could see two tiny lines of glass shards in the back of the Vulture's hand.

Lined up in a circular fashion; they had the appearance
of sharks teeth still fixed in their killers mouth. The gun
went off; carelessly, its flight finding purchase in the
plastic and wood frame of the French doors. More glass
showered forth, spraying Sabian's black desert boots.
Sabian moved away from the Vulture, tucking himself
in a corner and edging himself to his feet. He had recognised the pistol in the Vultures grip as being an early
1900 limited five chamber revolver, similar to the ham-
merless version made by Smith and Wesson. The Vulture had already used up five shots. Sabian with this
knew he just had the man to deal with; his gun was
nothing more now than a toy. Did he have another
weapon secretly concealed in a covert scabbard, harness
or pocket? Sabian thought the odds were against it. The
pistol he was currently using was generally held to be a
back up piece. Sabian surmised that vulture had lost his
main weapon in an earlier combat situation, perhaps
with Charlotte; more likely Brunner. The barrel of the
pistol was pointing at Sabian who studied it passively
and then fixed his gaze on the Vulture's eyes. They appeared to be closing with a look of deep pain spreading
across his face. The Vulture abruptly thumped his own
chest, coughing deeply and letting out an almost in-
audible moan. The pistol clicked, its small chamber
rotating and clicking once again; click click: two more
just for bad luck. Sabian remained expressionless.

"Only five chambers in that model I'm afraid dear
fellow!" Said Sabian.

The Vulture seemed unconcerned. He was still clutching his chest and repeatedly squeezing the trigger. Sabian
slowly and confidently stood and approached him,
cupping his hands around the pistol and taking it from

his weak and trembling grip. Sabian looked dispassion-
ately at the sweaty piece of black smoking metal.

"As I thought, a relic. They surely don't issue these
things to you do they?" He flicked the chamber open;
five empty shells. Just as he thought. Sabian took hold of
the Vulture's lapel and pulled the sweating greasy mass
toward him, slipping the pistol into the jackets inside
pocket. It was damp and soggy. The smell of cheap after-
shave mixed with old stale pies made Sabian crunch his
nose up for a second.

"Keep it; it will make a very amusing and novel
paperweight!" Vulture made no response, his breathing
now light and fast. Sabian pushed him lightly against his
sternum and he tottered back against the verandas thin
low wall. Blood was now running in rivulets from the
small rows of sharks teeth on the back of Vulture's hand.
His eyes were bloodshot and rapidly fading from the
world. He tried to speak, his voice barely a whisper.
Sabian moved closer.

"What was that dear fellow, what did you say?"

"I have a man on Brunner as we speak Sabian!"
Sabian's nose was almost touching the shinny slopes of
the Vultures.

"You know you are dying don't you?" whispered
Sabian. No response came. "Perhaps I can speed the
process up for you." With that Sabian started to push
hard against Vulture's sternum and with his free hand,
hooked his fingers under his sturdy leather belt and
proceeded to lift. He knew he would be more than
slightly foolish to think he would be able to lift his full
bulk without causing himself a serious injury of sorts.
His own ribs were still smarting, but nothing like they
were before. Adrenalin was probably at work, and when

it wore off again, it was going to hurt like hell. Sabian felt sure of that.

"My god, what are you doing?" Said Vulture.

"Helping you with your journey; just being a gentle-man." Sabian knew that due to the size of the bulk in front of him that it wouldn't take much to cause his upper body to act like an uneven seesaw on a low fulcrum and take the bird of prey over the edge.

"You wouldn't Mister Sabian. You are a true English-man."

Sabian spat back, the first time with emotion in his low guttural voice, "You got it right a few minutes ago when you could smell the scent of an assassin. That is what I do: I'm an assassin." Another push and lift set the seesaw on the fulcrum in motion.

"…and I do it particularly well!" as Sabian placed his right index finger in the middle of Vulture's forehead and pushed indignantly causing the seesaw to reach critical mass over its tipping point. Soundlessly at first he fell, followed by a high pitched scream that was quickened by the abruptness of the concrete and tiling below. Sabian was already turning and leaving the room.

13

Two Weeks Earlier in London

Dacres sat in the cold conference room studying the six serious faced delegates in the high backed chairs. There was a distinguishable disquiet in the room as a remote projector screen slid out of a slit in the ceiling some feet behind his head. The lights dimmed.

"Gentlemen we all know why we are here!" He said. A woman in a black pencil skirt and business jacket began to hand out six orange folders to the delegates one by one placing them onto the oval granite table next to their bottles of mineral water and complimentary ties and handkerchiefs. A beam from a rear wall cut the darkness and an image of a chemical formula hit the screen.

Dacres continued "Gentlemen the formula you see before you is the recently discovered ingredient of the Marimba Spheres." Another image snapped onto the screen showing half a dozen spheres in a black military cargo case.

"You will all be pleased to know we have had a team of scientists from around the world working tirelessly on this project, and we have now cracked the Marimbas' internal chemical secrets. This was the result of a consignment intervention in Prague by one of or agents." Each of the delegates continued to study the screen and the silhouette of Dacres moving mouth as their individual earpieces chattered in their ears like a small blizzard of flies in the room. Each fly speaking a different language to his neighbour. Dacres went on "The spheres contain a complex and hard to find compound."

He momentarily glanced from the screen which was now showing images of men in white gowns and full face masks handling the cargo case in a sterile refrigerated room. He passively indicated with his finger "As your dossiers will point out." There then followed a five minute silent film of the same men in gowns slowly taking a sphere from the case and subjecting it to a barrage of tests, weight, dimensions and temperature were just three of the readings logged into a book and computer onscreen. Constant glances were made by gowned individuals toward the large green LED digital temperature readout in the sterile environment. Glances were nervous and more frequent as the film went on and finally concluded with one of the spheres being deliberately punctured by a specially made machine which drained the blue gel out into a filter system. Dacres went on "There are as you know a large number of these spheres in the possession of some highly dangerous individuals and cell networks around the world. There are many more in unfinished states just waiting for the green light." A number of delegates looked at each other in puzzlement at the last statement from Dacres. He scanned their faces of bemusement and coughed, continuing "When they get the go ahead!" Several heads nodded with flies buzzing again in unison. One of the delegates, a Chinese man in his late fifties spoke in broken English. "Is it right you have an agent in Mauritius?"

"Yes, Mauritius for those of you that don't know has been discovered to be the place where the internal gel of the Marimba is manufactured. I have a man there; yes. It is his mission to try and contaminate the consignment currently in manufacture there; and more importantly to corrupt their mainframe which is sharing information of these spheres worldwide. It is hoped that he will plant a very successful Trojan Horse into the heart of any terrorist organisation that tries to access any information regarding the Marimba."

"What if he not successful?"

"That gentlemen does not bare thinking about!" He scanned their faces again and continued "It is more than anticipated that these things are now well within the hands of various terrorist networks. There is virtually nothing we can do about that except use our best and most competent operatives in the field to gather intelligence on moves afoot." The pencil skirted lady walked around the table pouring a fresh glass of water for each delegate as they remained transfixed on Dacres. "From our extensive research we now firmly believe that the Marimba Sphere has a predictable shelf life after manufacture and final sealing. If they are not used within a two month period of the finishing process there power starts to fade; they become nothing more than rather amusing and annoying firecrackers; that is if you don't mind a bit of flying glass as well." Nervous laughter then followed. "The Marimba in its normal stable state must be kept refrigerated for that state to remain; anything approaching body temperature for even a slightly extended period, say five to seven minutes will render the thing totally unstable and through minuet secretions from the host it will mean inevitable and imminent death for at least that individual; innocent carrier or otherwise." Another delegate leant forward and spoke in a broad Australian accent "How confident are you that the undercover operatives will be able to stop this?"

"You've got to realise ladies and gents that these are small groups of operatives that have infiltrated highly dangerous and organised cells. Their main job is reconnaissance and to report back. Reporting back has been somewhat a tricky affair. These cells are extremely sophisticated in the surveillance of their individual members. We recently received a report of a suspected cell member being a military intelligence operative. He was of course nothing of the sort. It didn't stop him having his throat cut whilst asleep."

"But that would suggest that they weren't that sophisticated?" The Australian delegate droned. Dacres raised an eyebrow in his direction the whites of his teeth slowly exposing. He then spoke slightly louder and indignantly. "No what it does demonstrate is there unwavering commitment to your death once a seed of doubt has been planted. Let me continue ladies and gents. These operatives have been cast to the four corners of this planet and we can only but trust their judgements, discretion and ability to get to us the intelligence that we need for our enforcement agencies. The job of enforcement is not for the operatives. They are the active eyes and ears of the intelligence community if you will. They are certain protocols which they must follow; especially when they think they have been compromised. I am not prepared to discuss these standard operating procedures in this forum. None of you have security clearance to the required level of that particular disclosure."

An American with a deep south accent leant forward "What about the rumour circulating in the surveillance community that an operative recently turned native and may have even joined a cells cause? Are we cleared for that sort of disclosure?" Dacres looked angry, displeased and tired. He took a sip of water thinking momentarily about the hand he played the previous evening in The St James Club, wishing he was there savouring the taste of a burnt oak vintage whisky and lighting up a stout Havana. He took a breath and continued, "Please I can not discuss these issues with you here! You have to remember these are deep cover operatives; they have to immerse themselves in these groups that they are sent to infiltrate. They must for all intents and purpose become one of that particular group. There is always a danger that they will somehow turn native. People are people. No amount of training and prior allegiance can stop it in some circumstances. People build bonds and friendships that are beyond the scope of their experience, training and better judgement. They probably never ever envisaged such a preposterous notion before embarking on work of this nature, that's why we do give prior awareness training and carry out psychological profiling on all our potential candidates. What is important beyond anything else ladies and gents is that we give these volunteer men and women, because that is what they are; our full and enduring support." There was a strained silence that followed as the lights came slowly up to the reception of screwed up eyes and faces. The projector screen slid back into its slot.

"Anyone for Baccarat?" Dacres said softly. The delegates eyed each other up in confusion.

"Thought not!"

14

Filling in time before Death

Sabian quickly checked the room number on the Palm hotel door. Room 903. Taking Bianco's brass fob from his pocket he made a mental note- 203. He sprinted toward the staircase, the fire in his chest now a smouldering funeral pyre.

Once at 203 he furtively checked around himself. He made sure both the hair and melted wax were still in one piece across the canyon of the door and frame. It looked perfect; textbook. He inserted the key and entered. The room was quiet and still. The soft smell of Paris perfume hung in the air; a popular brand with Bianco. The French door to the veranda was slightly ajar and the wail of sirens could be heard in the distance. A slight breeze caressed the silk curtains moving them with the subtleness of an apparitions hand. Sabian walked swiftly to the mini-bar; opening it he greedily took out a small tin of barley wine and placed it on the top of the vanity unit. He removed another can and shook it gently, and then unscrewing the bottom he removed a mobile phone and small black piece of hardware the size of a regular matchbox. Installing the Bluetooth connection he sat back in the chair cracking open the other can and gulping the contents down into the back of his throat. The matchbox device projected the image of a full size QWERTY keyboard using a laser from its small lens onto the flat table surface. Rummaging around in his dusty trouser pocket he took out the pink memory stick and inserted it into the side of the phone. The word PANASONIC fleetingly danced on the small organic crystal display of the phone then vanished. It was replaced by the grainy image of a blue Marimba Sphere. Sabian pressed the cancel button on the phone. A green cursor flickered above bold text announcing NEW FILE. His fingers approached the ghostly fiery red virtual keyboard. He hesitated, his fingers hovering. Throwing himself back into the chair he stared at the ceiling. Reaching into the breast pocket of his shirt he took out a battered packet of cigarettes and a brown and steel coloured lighter. He ran his thumb over the flying v emblem on its side and along its sleek raised fin. His lighter had been through a lot with him. It bore the scars of every scrape. He tossed it into the air a number of times. Throwing a cigarette into his mouth he lit it. He sucked deeply, the white paper drawing back over the greying charcoal like a receding tide just before a tsunami. Drawing on it several times he did not want to think about anything else; just living for the moment. He could die any time imminently. The door could burst open and he could be shot by an unknown or known assassin; he could be arrested; he could die of internal injuries. He did not care. The power of now was upon him. It was all consuming. He always felt totally alive in the face of imminent termination, his every sense and sinew ticking in the now, a total consuming realisation of existence. It made him think about all those times in ones life that held a comfortable numbness. That wasn't living. It was just filling in time before death. He took another long lingering drag and watched as the smoke spiralled drifting upward and toward the eddy currents of the open French doors. He triggered the Ronsons' flame several times contemplating the dance and danger of each burst, then with the flick of his accustomed wrist slid it back into the darkness of his breast pocket. He started typing immediately a message to London.

1 5

One Week Earlier- Peter Brunner

Peter Brunner was already on foot and running toward the Palm. The explosion was his worst nightmare come true. He had met up with Joseph Sabian and Charlotte Mercedes some six days earlier. As an Inspector for New Scotland Yards Anti-Terrorist Branch he had formed part of the link with this reconnaissance team. His brief from the Gold Group meeting was to work in close partnership with the intelligence services and pass on anything and everything when it was safe to do so.

Brunner, thirty eight, three years younger than Sabian and eight older than Charlotte had been a police officer for some seventeen years, the last three at the Yard. He had served in both uniform and CID. Divorced and without children he was the ideal candidate for the secondment. A chance to see the world. He met Sabian the previous week at an open roadside bar along a stretch of dusty road leading into Grand Baie. He had approached Sabian who was sat with his back to him and slowly sipping on a Black Russian from cocktail glass with a light dusting of salt around its rim. He was sat on a high bar stool and the only person there. Sabian was enjoying the high afternoon sun that was beating a pleasant rhythm onto his back. Brunner recognised him from an earlier briefing photograph from the Joint Committee Gold Group at MI6 headquarters several days earlier. He was also in the right part of the neighbourhood. Brunner took up a bar stool next but one along from Sabian ordering a bottle of Kronenberg from the lone barman. Sabian did not look once in his direction even fleetingly. Brunner took a sip from his frosted glass, ice clinking and popping in the tropical heat. He removed something from his pocket and then opened a black leather wallet containing his police identification warrant card. It displayed a large silver coloured metal crest opposite his photograph mounted behind a hologram of the Metropolitan Police crest. He was about to move it toward Sabian. "Put it away!" Brunner hesitated with the comment and then snapped it shut slipping it nervously back into his trouser pocket. Sabian had been surveying his new contact in a piece of glass at the back of the bar between a twisted ornate bottle of some European bier and Vermouth shot glass. He recognised Brunner from a JPEG encrypted email he had been sent by his office the previous evening. Sabian continued to talk without looking at Brunner. "Want to get us both killed? I suggest you leave that thing somewhere out of the way. May I suggest not your hotel safe or anywhere in the room for that matter. Bury the thing on the beach tonight or weight it down in the water with a marker." "Sorry- I'm Brunner—Peter Brunner." His voice was nervous and uncertain.

"Yes I know who you are, not here. Let's take a walk." Sabian finished his drink gulping the last mouthful and licked the salt from his lips. Sabian looked at Brunner properly for the first time offering his right hand. "Sabian, Joseph Sabian but you can call me Joe!" Brunner glanced at the outstretched hand and reluctantly shook it. "You should loosen up a bit more" continued Sabian as he started to walk past Brunner along the sandy path. Brunner followed. The water of the bay glistened blues and purples as the suns rays reflected a hundred sparkling diamonds on its surface as the two men walked along the bay path. Several luxury yachts were moored nearby. Sabian walked silently and this made Brunner extremely uncomfortable. Without warning Sabian hopped onto a narrow boarding plank flanked by two low rope supports as rails to a medium sized cruiser. He jumped aboard the Calista, as did Brunner. Stepping down into the spacious cabin Sabian turned toward him. "What do you think the anti-terrorist branch can add to this mission Mr Brunner?" Brunner had a puzzled expression on his face his eyes flicking to the left as a double set of cabin saloon swing doors twitched. Brunner could clearly make the outline out of a woman silhouetted against the far wall of the connecting room above the doors. Sabian's eyes followed the same path. "Charlotte you can come out" said Sabian. A brief moment later Charlotte Mercedes emerged into the light. Sabian detected the slightest hint of chemistry as Brunner's eyes fleetingly scanned the length of her body, toe to head. She diverted her gaze, her hands behind her back with her left foot pointing toward Peter.

"Anyone for coffee?" said Sabian.

16

The Calista

Peter, Charlotte and Joseph took up seats on the Calistas upper deck. The water lapped lightly at the stern. Peter sipped his white coffee. Joe took his black and strong. Charlotte drank a glass of iced tea. She stole several sideway glances at Peter who was sat wooden and inappropriately dressed with a shirt and tie. The light fabric of his shirt clinging to his torso, he felt like a vacuum sealed product on a supermarket shelf. Charlotte leant forward. The subtle swell of her breasts pushed against the light frayed denim top. Peter reciprocated the glances as she fixed her gaze over the rim of her glass. He stiffened his back and looked more wooden than ever. She momentarily licked her upper lip and then slapped her glass down hard on the table. Peter jumped.

"As I said earlier, you really do need to loosen up!" Sabian reiterated.

"No, no I'm fine. The sooner we get down to the business of this whole damn thing the be ….."

Sabian continued cutting Brunners last word off "No, I think you need to relax, believe me! At the moment you look like a paedophile in a prep school. You will need to relax so as to blend in with the locals and the pace around here. You are quite clearly not doing that at the moment my dear fellow!" Brunner did not respond. He shifted his gaze between the two of them and fleetingly at Charlotte's cleavage. She shuffled uncomfortably back in her seat pulling the denim of her top in a protective manner. Not that it made much difference. Brunner cleared his throat "Where is everyone staying?" Charlotte spoke with a soft middle England accent with a sharp brittle undercurrent timbre, "Joes' is up the beach. He'll show you later. I'm at the Palm Hotel as I understand you are too. This boat is just somewhere where we can get our heads together. It belongs to Maurice Longinner. He works with the French Embassy and is our main contact out here. He is also our liaison with the local authority and police."

Sabian continued "We are on relatively safe ground here on this vessel. I am told by the Quartermasters back in London that it is crammed full of state of the art counter surveillance equipment, bug hunters, cloaking devices and radar jammers. That sort of thing if you catch my drift?" Brunner nodded. Sabian poured himself another thick black coffee and gulped the luke warm offering back. "And another thing" he went on, "if you have a mobile phone dump it along with your badge. It's just another Achilles heel that we can't afford to be exploited." Brunner was watching Sabian's mouth move and nodding his head in slow deliberate agreement. "I take it from the stark absence of luggage that you've already checked in?" Charlotte chipped in. "Yeah about two hours ago. Thought it was important I find the two of you first before I considered anything else though."

"Your luggage, where is it now?" said Sabian. "There's nothing sensitive in there if that's what you're worried about. Just clothing and toiletries. No documents or equipment!" Charlotte leant forward, the swell of her breast rising again. "Mr Brunner" she said, "We can not afford any slip ups. Normal everyday communication we can not and must not use. All your coms must come through us. It is highly likely that the cell operating out here may have cottoned onto the fact that something is wrong. There are two deep cover operatives working amongst them and we have heard absolutely nothing from the two of them for over a week now. We have however been told of a possible location for the manufacturing plant for the blue gel, that all important ingredient of the Marimba. It is not too far from here; and hence we must exercise the utmost caution at all times in our pursuit. We must be nothing more than a mirage in the desert of their radar or not appear on it at all. If any of us do not meet at pre-arranged rendezvous the others must be completely familiar with their role and what is expected of them without having to rely on phones or other communicators. We have certain encrypted equipment at the Palm and we've been issued with pens that can take JPEG images and that's about it. You have got a small personal issue of kit that I will run through with you later which you may find useful!" Brunner thought he could see her nipples becoming erect through the tight denim. His eyes fell to her cleavage on several occasions, where a heavy ruby pendant hung.

17

Charlotte Mercedes

Charlotte Mercedes had been with her department only eighteen months. She had previously graduated from Leicestershire University in politics and social sciences. She had moved to a maisonette just off the Fulham High Road to keep an old girlfriend company after ending a particularly miserable relationship. She had never intended to find work in the capital.

An advertisement in the free Times paper on the Underground had caught her eye. And so she became a number crunching clerk with MI6 the following March. A short notice slot had developed and here she was. It seemed like an opportunity not to be missed. She had never heard of Joseph Sabian until the preliminary assignment meeting of the Gold Committee Joint Group.

Her brief for the mission had been simple. She as far as possible was not to get involved other than at the specific request of Sabian. She was responsible for the maintenance, archiving and sending of all encrypted messages. If anything happened to him she was not meant to act as his substitute but to get on the first available plane back to London regardless of her frame of reference.

Sabian was not impressed, he normally worked alone. He said as much the second night after their familiarisation course. They took a light lunch just off Covent Garden and then went to The Moon Under The Water for a couple of drinks then back to The St James Club where Dacres had reserved two single rooms. Sabian had forgotten the reservation chitty the finance and resources department had put together with the necessary authorisation code. It was a singularly embarrassing moment where Sabian found himself fumbling through his pockets in the presence of a concierge half his age. Sabian relented and in the end used his Country Gentleman's Association membership card to negotiate a discount with the intention of filing a claim for the difference later. The bar area had been empty. The air conditioning was on full. The heat outside had been totally stifling almost like there was no air and no breeze to talk about. Especially that last stretch up Jermyn Street. The bar was just heaven; a welcome break in the madness of the last few hours.

They synchronised and meshed together like a well oiled piece of machinery. They picked at Pistachio nuts and popcorn served on sterling silver platters by the white topped barman between drinks. When it was time to leave for their rooms Charlotte had threaded her arm around his as they entered the elevator. Sabian at first felt reticent. He tried like a gentleman to place her on her bed and cover her whilst she was still fully clothed. He had only removed her high heels and placed them neatly by the dresser. As he pulled away from her she put her right arm heavily around his neck and pulled him like a dull weight toward her face. Her breath smelt of peppermint and vodka. Her skin smelt of clean fresh soap and Paris perfume. She grinned and her brown eyes locked with his. He was aware that she was tugging at some of her own clothing. He looked down and saw that she was lifting her skirt. "Charlotte I must ...."

"Shhhhhhhh!" she breathed and motioned with her free left hand against her lips.

"Loook!!" she said. Sabian glanced down at the soft mounds of her flesh and did not hold back; could not hold back.

It had become an increasing trend of the Joint Committee to have a back up buddy arrangement. Sabian had increasingly found fringe benefits in this new policy!

18

Cheap Chaffing Sandals

Sixty five minutes later Peter Brunner was back at the Calista waiting patiently sporting a flecked blue and red Hawaiian shirt desert shorts and beach sandals that were already starting to chafe the inside of his feet near his big toes. He glanced momentarily at his wrist watch as a large black four door saloon glided soundlessly to a halt beside him as he placed a blue baseball cap on his head. The heat of the sun was already smarting his thinly covered scalp. His arms and upper legs had also begun to tingle in the absence of sun lotion protection. The drivers window glided open to a half way position equally without sound.

A small man with olive black skin spoke with a high French accent. "The Captain's Launch, yes??" A welcome gust of ice-cold refrigerated air made contact with Brunner's chest as he walked toward the car. Brunner nodded in acknowledgement as he opened the rear passenger door and slid in onto the cold leather seat. Ice cold air pumped through vents in the middle console unit of the seat and on the floor forcing a soft blanket of kindness over the reddening flesh of his feet as they shuffled and scraped against the hard unfinished plastic of his sandals. It was such heaven. The car set off.

A light ethnic tune played at low volume with bongos and wailing; lightly accompanied by a haunting sitar and mandolin. The car glided like a hovercraft on through Grand Baie toward a spiral of narrowing back streets. There was a smell of fresh oranges with the hint of pine. A traffic light type air freshener danced below the drivers rear view mirror. Below that hung a small clear crystal skull with red gem stone eyes. It swivelled several times on a fishbone link silver metal chain and then seemed to steady looking back at Brunner and winking as the high suns rays drenched the mirror and dashboard area. The driver did not speak. Neither did Brunner. The silence felt comfortable. The skull winked again!

Moving through the spider network of back streets the pleasant tourist atmosphere of the Bay slowly dissipated. The suns light was cut off by high trees and vegetation. The odd mud hut and sheet metal handmade makeshift home flashed by. Hypnotic flashes of light hammered momentarily through breaks in the upper greenery. The driver still did not speak.

As they approached a widening junction in the road Brunner's attention was drawn to a group of five men in their mid to late twenties stood by a burnt out car on its roof. Each stared at their passing car with an angry aggressive look in their eyes. The upturned car smouldered. It appeared dead. A big game animal had been caught in the wilderness and they were about to plunder its flesh. The unblinking gaze of the five pairs of eyes followed them as they passed through the intersection. The driver did not regard them. Not even for a moment.

The crystal skull remained fixed on Brunner. Its now dull red sunken eyes were that of a corpse staring up from a mortuary slab. Brunner glanced back at the intersection and thought what he saw looked like a human arm sticking out of the drivers window of the upturned car. The image stood for a micro second but was snapped from view by one of the males who blocked his line of vision approaching the door. But he wasn't really sure what he had seen, if anything! Brunner straightened looking forward with a sudden feeling of being watched. The driver's eyes were looking at him via the rear view mirror. "They're no trouble. Just kids. Pay no attention to them!"

19

The Captain's Launch

Twenty minutes into the journey the car came to a stop outside an open plan restaurant on a raised platform above the Bays glistening blue water. Brunner asked the driver how much his fare was and he responded by waving his left hand slowly, "Already taken care of, already taken care of!" Brunner tried to offer him a tip with an unknown value currency note. The driver would not accept as Brunner tried to exit the vehicle. "No wait!" the driver spat out. Brunner looked surprised and agitated. "You must wait for the guards, it is too dangerous!" It was then that Brunner saw the two uniformed security officers walking slowly and deliberately toward the taxi. Each wore a pale blue shirt with epaulettes and a flat cap with a gold shield affixed. With their black sidearms in holsters, they reminded Brunner of New York cops.

The rear door to the taxi was opened by the taller of the two as if he were a doorman at an expensive film premiere in Leicester Square. Neither spoke. He followed them to the entrance of the restaurant feeling like he was under arrest, walking silently between them, stressing over whether he should offer them a tip or not.

The fact that he did not understand the currency currently occupying his wallet just added to his anxiety. He chose not to say anything stepping up into the raised area of the restaurant floor. Both guards turned as he entered and continued their sentry post.

The restaurant was fairly empty. Sabian and Mercedes were sat at a rear corner table overlooking the water of the bay. Soft candles flickered in small white finger bowls on all the tables. A metal fluted wind chime hung from the ceiling playing a soft haunting tune as the breeze from the bay came in from the west. A couple in their forties sat looking longingly into each others eyes and at another table a local sat impatiently twisting himself around and glancing at his watch periodically.

"Ah good to see you", said Sabian. Brunner pulled up a chair and sat. Charlotte did not look up and continued to survey the wine list. Sabian was dressed in a blue cotton collared shirt with the first two buttons undone. His sleeves were rolled up. He looked relaxed and casual yet smart. Brunner suddenly felt like the typical English tourist abroad sat there in his chaffing cheap sandals. Sabian's left foot was protruding from under the table and Brunner couldn't help but notice the smart shiny black buckled shoes.

Charlotte placed the wine list down in front of her and said without regarding Peter "What would you recommend Joe?" She was wearing a sober black dress with thin shoulder straps. It was less revealing than her earlier garment but Peter couldn't help but notice how the Lycra hugged in all the right places. Joseph glanced up at the maitre'de who came quickly and subserviently. "Got any Bollinger 57?" The man, a local spoke with a French accent but in impeccable English. "I'm afraid Mr

Sabian it was the last bottle you had two nights ago. We aren't expecting any more stock until the middle of next week." Sabian nodded and abruptly handed the wine list back. "I'll have a bourbon and branch water, no ice, got it?" Charlotte and Peter both stared at Sabian but still not at each other. The waiter nodded and gestured with his feet almost like he was clicking his heels. "And for the sir and the lady?" "I'll just have a small beer." Peter said. "And for you madam?" Charlotte momentarily glanced for the first time at Peter, almost as if for some support in the wake of Sabians' abruptness. "Same here!" she said. "A small beer for you to, yes??" "Yes, that's right, thanks." She again glanced at Brunner who was not looking in her direction and appeared to be massaging the ankle to his left foot, between that and fidgeting with a small silver pendant hanging around his sweaty neck.

Thirty seconds later and their drinks were being served. Sabian savoured the taste of the bourbon running his tongue over the slopes of his teeth as if trying to extract every taste opportunity from the mouthful. Charlotte and Peter were busy studying the menus as Sabian sat back in his chair and took another mouthful of the elixir. He didn't look at the menu but instead choose to stare out across the darkening bay and making occasional glances at the male sat by himself near the restaurant entrance. The waiter returned. "All ready to order?" Sabian sat sharply up "Yes, I'll have a turbot poche', sauce mousse line and half a roast partridge." Brunner shot a hard stare at Sabian and spoke firmly, "What about ladies first?" Charlotte turned to Sabian waiting for his response. Sabian with disinterest said "We'll have none of that here, do you understand, we are all equals here' our lives could depend on a certain discipline."

Brunner could not hold Sabians angered stare and glanced again at the heel of his right foot for some sort of meaningful distraction. Charlotte was similarly put off balance yet again. She looked over to Brunner and held his gaze for slightly more than the norm. Their eyes locked for a period of time somewhere between pleasant revelation of admiration and uncomfortableness. Both snapped their eyes away as the waiter approached. Charlotte looked up at the waiter who still stood like a statue with his pen poised over his frayed notebook. "I'll have breast of chicken, petite poi's and French fries with a side order of garlic bread." "Thank you madam, and you sir?" "Yes, I'll have the same." Said Brunner. Again the glance.

The meal continued for some fifty minutes mostly in silence, although it was despite Sabians' arrogance at the start of the evening a comfortable silence.

Brunner was ravenous. He had not eaten for about ten hours. The flight alone had been twelve hours from Heathrow. He had taken up an in flight meal at the start of his out ward bound journey, which had left him feeling somewhat queasy for the first several hours of his flight. He had had to make several excuse me's to the young boy and older woman sat next to him in row D. They had been very polite about letting him out of his window seat but the patience was starting to fray on the last occasion when he had to wake the old woman up, his bowels feeling like they were going to evacuate into the lap of the young boy playing with his Power Rangers figure.

Charlotte had been watching Brunner at several points. She had been watching the way he ate. He did not notice this. Sabian ate and made a number of observatory glances still at the local at the end table, who for all his waiting still had not ordered a meal or even a drink. The waiter had approached him on more than two occasions and had been waved off by the back of his hand. He was now checking his watch every two or three minutes and glancing nervously back over the shoulders of the security guards and up the dusty winding track that the locals took for a road.

20

Move It Blood!

Back at the intersection a number of bad things were underway. They had started the second after the black taxi containing Brunner and the dancing skull had passed through. Daemon Flagg thought he briefly saw a face, pale and white looking back at them as the car snaked past. Realising this he had promptly blocked the view of the arm that had fallen limply out onto the dusty road. Once the black car was gone out of sight he cruelly stamped on the hand to the sound of cracking bones and a piercing inhuman scream. He laughed, his weather beaten black olive skin looking like leather in contrast to his pearly white teeth and the single gold front tooth. The other four members of his posse jeered nervously and apprehensively waited for Flaggs next move. The fingers of the mans hand looked twisted and deformed as he tried to retract the damaged limb back into the safe confines of the upturned car. His groans went on and on. Flagg grew agitated and impatient at this and took out the silver automatic handgun from the waistband of his khaki shorts. He took out the empty clip and threw it to the ground. Fumbling for several seconds he took from his back pocket another clip. This one was full. He slapped it hard as it penetrated the guns ivory grip. He took aim standing on what was left of the lower arm to prevent his prey from escaping. He fired twice in quick succession. The hand exploded into five pieces leaving just a stump at the wrist. The arm went limp as blood projected about three feet out on to the dusty road. The blood quickly turned to a dirty brown paste as it mixed with the sand and oil on each of its networked spidery courses. The groans had gone quiet.

Dudsley was holding a gold wrist watch against his arm and comparing it to the one already firmly attached to his wrist. He cocked his head from side to side a number of times trying to decide if it was going to make a suitably acquired replacement. Flagg walked past him nudging his shoulder deliberately. "It's a fake. Or else it would be on my wrist now!" Dudsley appeared momentarily hurt by the comment of their leader who had already started to walk toward the large wooden hut just in the mouth of the woods. "Bring them both!" He demanded.

The four then began to drag the man and woman from the car. Both were unconscious. Their heads bobbed dipped and twisted on the axis of each of their necks as they were dragged by their feet along the craggy stony path toward the hut.

There was a mounting smell of manure in the air as they neared the hut as Flagg had uncoupled the large wooden beam restrainer from the double wooden doors cracking them open to a slither. "Oh Jesus Christ, boss?" said Alvin dropping one of the woman's legs. "That smell is too much man!" chipped in Donny as he gripped both nostrils with his free hand.

Flagg was not amused. He walked toward Alvin suck-ing his teeth and caressing the ivory grip of his gun in his waistband. "Move it blood!" he threatened with his neck craned and his face almost touching his.

The four dragged the two into the hut. They gagged and coughed at the high stench. The two unconscious victims, who had up to then been out of it, were starting to come to. The man continued to groan with a low guttural noise in the back of his throat. The woman started to shake her head in slow rhythmic dances as if being woken up by someone flashing a phial of smelling salts under her nose.

Flagg seemed unmoved by the smell that the others thought they could each taste in their mouths. Alvin looked across at Flagg who had his back to the group and was surveying a large aluminium chute with a three foot pile of manure at the bottom. There were about a dozen, maybe more of similar piles around the large shed. Alvin had tears running down his face and his eyes were stinging, "Why here boss?" He said. Flagg looked back and promptly paced toward him. For a brief moment he thought Flagg was going to punch him. He flinched as Flagg ran his fingers aggressively over his left cheek capturing the wetness in his fingers and rubbing its velvety texture between his index finger and thumb. "Nancy boy!" he spat out and followed the manoeuvre up with a sharp dig to Alvin's left shoulder causing him to topple back onto the manure stained floor. The others laughed nervously and Donny half turned away feeling a salty wetness invade his own lips and mouth.

Alvin strained to his feet as the laughter was dying around him. His hands, arms and upper legs were caked in brown thick stains. He stood half shocked and half bemused at the mess he had become.

Flagg stood looking at them, his legs astride, one arm behind his back the other masturbating the ivory texture of his gun. "Gentlemen…" he paused surveying their faces for further signs of weakness, like a general before giving the order to advance or a 'tally ho and over the top boys.' He continued "The smell of their decaying flesh will not go noticed around here, their bodies will soon enough turn to the same shit that we are going to bury them in." He ran his index finger along the trigger guard of his gun and continued. "I've used this method before you will not be surprised to here!"

"I want them tied to those low tables in case they come round. I don't like scenes!"

They dragged the man to a low two foot bench made of battered stained wood and started to tie his ankles to the contraption with some thin binding rope that Flagg threw to them from his waistband.

The man groaned as full consciousness invaded his being. His eyes opened as Flagg pushed Donny out of the way and in a single motion shot the bound man between his eyes. The back of his head exploded like a water melon, a red shower flushing the floor beneath and spattering a nearby wall. The group fell silent and motionless as Flagg motioned with his pistol to the woman.

"Tie her and then strip her. Do it now! I don't like fucking dead things!"

Several minutes later the young woman was stripped and shackled to another low bench. She was still not fully conscious. Her cool pale marble like structure and flesh contrasted sharply with the bench and its surroundings. Flagg took hold of her left breast kneading it like dough leaving a brown stained imprint. She groaned momentarily as he placed his gun down and started to undo the clasp on his shorts. He glanced back at the others. They stood frozen and perplexed yet with greedy expressions. "You!" Flagg spat out indicating to Donny. "Come here nancy boy!" Donny approached hesitatingly as Flagg roughly pulled down his faded denim shorts.

Donny stood there with his limp penis eyeing up Flagg's gun that he had placed down on the outcrop of aluminium from the nearby chute. He felt powerless to act in his defence, yet the gun was only an arms length away and closer to him than it was to Flagg.

Flagg pushed him away and turned from him laying astride the woman he motioned rhythmically on top of her several times groaning, "You got a mighty fine body bitch, hell yeah!" The woman started to heave and buck under him as she gave out an ear piercing scream. Flagg followed this up by forcing his shorts into her mouth as his hips danced a faster rhythm to an abrupt and shaking stillness.

He continued to ram the shorts into her mouth, her eyes bulging helplessly. He took a step back from her and removed the shorts. The hut filled with her screams of pain fear and loathing. Flagg wiped himself on the back of his khaki shorts and pulled them on. He was just about to clip the clasp to the front of his pants when a large silhouette of a man engulfed the opening of the hut. The posse all simultaneously turned to look as the figure took a step forward out of the backlit sun and into the dark shadowy environment. Flagg strained to focus his eyes on the features of the strangers face. Flagg's face then filled with a beaming smile of recognition. The womans screams had turned to sobs as she turned too to look at the figure.

Maurice Longinner stepped into the middle of the group as they drew naturally around him in a none threatening circle. He stood some six feet and seven inches, was dressed in a cream coloured cowboy hide jacket and trousers. A large cream Stetson graced his head and a boot lace tie with a cow horn metal adornment graced his neck.

"What you boys playin' at 'ere??" He said coldly and calmly as he surveyed the chaos of the room, first glancing at the exploded remains of the man's head and the female who was now staring at him and shaking and trying to speak but quite unable to do so.

He paced around the room a few moments. Every few feet he stopped and checked his immaculate white boots for signs of detritus and then continued his survey with his hands behind his back. All their eyes followed him as he came to stop by the woman.

He did not seem to see her nakedness. He looked at her face and into her eyes. She was crying and her eyes were scanning backwards and forwards at a frantic pace with total and absolute fear. Maurice leaned forward placing his large dry cracked left hand on her forehead. She closed her eyes and her face seemed to lose all tension. Her voice trembled and stuttered as she first soundlessly mouthed his name and in the next breath said his name, "Maurice".

He turned to face the group his hand still offering a moment of comfort in the madness of the ordeal that the woman had just been subjected to. Flagg took a step forward as if to offer a meaningless explanation and was stopped in his tracks by Maurice raising the front of his right hand up to him in protest. Flagg stood staring unable to speak. Unable to find words for the big man.

"I can't trust you to carry out simple orders!" Maurice droned staring at Flagg.

The woman's eyes started to open in terror. "Our secret service friends here are not toys for your amusement!" Flagg stood momentarily looking back at the others for some kind of support. Support was not coming from any of them as they all stood staring at the brown stains on the floor and becoming aware again of the stench in their nostrils.

The woman started sobbing and turned her head away from Maurice staring at the dark wooden slats as Maurice placed the barrel of Flagg's gun against her left temple and squeezed the trigger!

21

❦

The Bill Please!

The waiter came over to Sabian. "Everything alright sir?" Sabian was still studying the furtive character on the last table. "Yes,-yes, fine, can we have the bill now please?" he said scantly regarding the figure beside him. "Mister Sabian it has already been taken care of by Mister Longinner." Sabian focused a hard enquiring stare at the waiter and asked, "Is he around at the moment?" The waiter stole a fleeting glance with the stranger near the exit. Sabian continued "I would like to thank him for his excellent hospitality." Sabian with a flourish wiped the corners of his mouth that were totally clean with his napkin, scrunched it and tossed it like a rag into the middle of the table. Looking at Charlotte and Peter, Sabian spoke abruptly again, "Are we done?"

Both nodded in unison resigned to the idea that regardless of the idea of them being done or not they were. Sabian snapped his fingers, "Cab please!" Brunner shot him another hard stare and glanced at Charlotte who was rolling her eyes in disgust. The waiter nodded, a follow up act of subservience and made his way to a small exposed office area the size of a broom cupboard at the rear of the bar. Straining to read the number from a business card on the makeshift message board he lifted the heavy handset and started to dial a number. Sabian was straining to hear his conversation that was muffled and dull and trying to fill in blanks with some amateurish attempt at lip reading. The waiter had eye contact with Sabian and turned away leaving the back of his weather beaten bald head exposed.

"Come we must go!" said Sabian rising surveying Charlotte first and then Peter.

"Joe, what's wrong, why so edgy?" she whispered. Sabian was halfway across the restaurant as he gave a response "No time for answers, come we must make haste". The other two rose from the table and followed with slightly bewildered expressions on their faces. The waiter turned at the sudden activity, the phone now cradled on his right shoulder and blinked deliberately twice at the stranger on the end table. As the stranger began to stand Sabian cast him a sharp unexpected blow to the front of his windpipe with a chop from the straightened heel of his right hand. There was a guttural escape of air mixed with a double snapping noise as the figure dropped to his knees and then falling forward; his head sharply striking the back of a heavy wooden chair. The two security guards turned simultaneously reaching for their sidearms. Sabian lashed out with his right foot almost blindly catching one of them square in the middle of his back. He screamed something in French, his cocked gun going off, sending its round into the wildness of the night. The other guard was having trouble drawing his gun. It had somehow jammed itself into the holster. "Mon Dieu!"- his voice was alarmed and raised. His right hand appeared glued to the unmovable butt of his Luger. Sabian pushed him hard against his chest. He toppled to the ground as Sabian taking the lead started to run toward the water which was only several yards away.

The waiter was panicking and talking fast on the telephone. He put the receiver down and quickly joined the man with his broken neck and the two hapless guards who both still appeared dazed. "Look what you do to my customers and staff Mister Sabian!" he shouted after them as they sank below the surface of the bay and started to swim.

22

No time for Heavy Petting

The bay water was cool and fresh. Brunner discarded his sandals throwing them with contempt as he started to make deep strokes in the water. His feet had a tingling in them that washed its way through the rest of his body as the water invigorated his tired and jet-lagged limbs. The golden perfect circle of the sun had started to sink into the millpond of the bays furthest horizon. Brunner was a good swimmer, yet Sabian was trailblazing ahead at about twenty to thirty feet and Charlotte was swimming somewhere near Brunner's feet. His big toe had slightly caressed her left shoulder at least twice in about ten feet without complaint. Nine minutes later they had crossed the bay and pulled themselves upon to the small shelf of sand taking shelter behind a large rock. Both Peter and Charlotte lay on their backs trying to catch their breath. Sabian was on all fours' looking over the craggy rock, surveying the other side of the bay. He wasn't out of breath, not even slightly. Sure enough Sabian saw what he had been straining to see. The sudden rip of an outboard motor and a small two man boat leaving the jetty at the rear of the restaurant.

Peter's hand had fallen close to Charlottes, almost touching, so close that there was a sense of touching between them; each set of body heat aura intermingling with the next. Sabian stood, "Come no time for heavy petting, we're in real danger!" They scrambled to their feet and followed Sabian into the undergrowth where they ran for their lives; the leaves branches and foliage ripping at their flesh, smarting on initial contact but without significant pain as their adrenalin pumped hard through veins and arteries. Brunner ran bare foot and could no longer feel the balls of his feet. They had gone numb with pain. They had become nothing more than just instruments of transport to carry him to safety from mortal danger. After a solid five minutes of running they came to another opening in the woods leading to another stretch of water. Brunner squinted as a branch of heavy thorns catapulted toward his face nearly taking out his left eye and when he once again looked ahead saw a number of expensive white bodied yachts and speedboats moored on the other side in the clearing. He could just about make out the name of the Calista in the dimming light.

"Please Sabian what's happening? I can't do this anymore!" he insisted. Sabian did not speak wading into the ink of the water. Turning back he said, "Stay here and we're all dead, that's for sure!" Brunner with deep lines of resignation on his face waded into the water followed by Charlotte. He would have noticed had he looked back how her black Lycra dress, now wet and more hugging than ever was sucking at every line of her body, the bottom of the dress firmly tucked into her black camisole knickers. In the fading light she looked naked, but Brunner did not look back and if he had done so would not have cared or stolen a second glance. Again they swam.

Once at the Calista Sabian half shimmied up the rope ladder clinging to the bow whilst the others remained in the water. Brunner slipped his head under the black ink of the water emerging and flicking the hair out of his eyes. "What the fuck was all that about; the fucking marathon?" he spat spraying water from his mouth. "Shhhh!" Sabian motioned with a finger against his lips as a black Sedan with diplomatic plates and two French embassy flags fluttering either side of its bonnet drew to a halt beside the Calista. Sabian continued, "We've been sold out. I'm pretty sure of it. It's Longinner, that's his car. He shouldn't even be here!"

Charlotte's face was pale, her make up washed out along with the blackness of her eye liner now gone. Her hair was wet and lank as she trembled in the now cold of the water her bottom lip quivering, her cheeks lightly fluttering. Sabian was craning and chadding several feet up the rope ladder watching the sedan as four men emerged from it. Peter ducked his head under the water a second time.

The big man Longinner had stood up straight from the front passenger seat placing the large Stetson onto his head and walked toward the Calista. He did not look back at the others. He did not seek or need their approval. Three males followed the chief, two of them laughing and nudging each other, a third walked slightly ahead of them and behind Longinner. The third male was not laughing. He walked staring at the ground and had one hand firmly resting on the ivory grip of a pistol in his waistband.

After several minutes of the knocking of internal doors, abused crockery and raised dull meaningless voices the four men emerged from the Calista. They walked silently toward the parked Sedan, the man with the ivory pistol breaking the silence with "Not there boss!" as he slipped into the darkness of the rear of the car. The big man had cast him an evil cutting glance in the rear view mirror as he neatly placed his Stetson down on his lap and ordered the driver to drive. The car abruptly did a searing tyre melting u turn tearing up the dust in the road as it went back the direction it had came from. Sabian shimmied up the remaining third of the rope ladder. "Both of you stay here, I'll be back in a moment." He pulled himself onto the deck once he was sure that there was no danger of the car coming back and its rear reds had vanished into a winding back road through a wooded outcrop. He entered the cabin of the boat.

He was quickly back on the deck holding onto a sand coloured rucksack with two small blue flotation tanks attached to it. He slung the pack over his back threading his arms though the thick weaving of the arm restrainers and slinked back down the ladder into the now icy cold of the water. "Come we need to swim again!" Brunner and Mercedes did not have the inclination or energy to argue. They swam through the black inky looking water as the sun collapsed from view. Sabian looked like a badly fallen parachutist as he swam with the pack uncomfortably purchased between his shoulder blades and lower back.

For about fifteen minutes they swam at a steady pace following the contour of the bay away from the Calista and on the opposite side from The Captain's Launch. Sabian gradually peeled from the contour of the shoreline followed by the others out to a small island about five hundred feet out into the bay. It was during this unexpected diversion that Charlotte developed crushing cramps in her right calf and vanished under the water. Coughing and spluttering she emerged gasping for breath, a fast tight rattle in the back of her throat as she tried to draw air in through the spasm of her throat muscles; she spayed Brunner with her frantic arm wheeling. Sabian threw the rucksack to Brunner who unexpecting its dull weight vanished under the water for a split second until the two flotation tanks corrected the situation. Brunner emerged spitting salty water and fighting with the webbing to get his arms through it. Sabian instinctively had dived several feet under Charlotte bringing her to the surface and forcing her onto her back where her breathing relaxed somewhat and evened out in rhythm. Sabian swam with her in this position to the small island, his legs lightly kicking under hers and his right hand supporting her chin with her head resting against his chest. Her eye's stared off into the vastness of the universe as the blood tinged moon appeared as a feint image of a mirage in the hot desert sun.

Peter dragged himself onto the sand, the bag now a dead weight on his back. Sabian dragged Charlotte. The three lay for what seemed like an hour, catching breath and unable to move the heaviness of their limbs.

2 3

Joe You've Thought of Everything!

Sabian was the first to reanimate himself by opening the rucksack that Brunner had come to despise so much. He removed from the wet webbing bag a black military waterproof cargo freight type box. He clicked it open and threw two packets from inside toward Peter and Charlotte. "Put these on or you're both going to die of hyperthermia otherwise!"

Once inside the foil space blankets they started gradually to feel human again. Brunner was suddenly reminded of the pains in his feet; each blister and cut taking on a new life of its own. Sabian was still rummaging through the contents of the military freight box. "What are you doing?" enquired Brunner. Sabian explained, "I put these together some time ago. Though they are basic kits you'll find the items useful. Here put these on!" Sabian held out two wrist watches. Peter protested, "But I've got a watch." He looked fleetingly at his watch. A water bubble floated where it shouldn't between the face and the crystal. It had stopped some twenty minutes ago. "Oh" he moaned. Charlotte took

7 3

her watch reluctantly. "But these are men's watches, that won't fit around my wrist." Sabian snapped an identical watch onto his left wrist. Sabian took her watch back, "You can adjust the band like this." He gave her the watch back. With the click of the security clasp it fit perfectly. "The quartermasters at HQ gave me these." He went on. "They're Ingersoll Navigators, the black spider PVD coated version with modified Cyan seven watt LED's." Sabian pressed a button on the side of his watch. Three steady blue lights clicked on from the face of the watch at the six, ten and two markers. Sabian kept his other hand cupped over the metal case. "One depression gives you blue lights; a second press gives you a SOS mode." Sabian pressed the button and the lights on his watch flickered the rhythm of an SOS signal. The light was only visible to them due to Sabian's cupped hand. "The lights can be seen for about a mile, a third press and you have a very powerful defence tool or torch." Sabian pressed the button again and three much brighter LED's lit. Brunner and Mercedes were temporarily blinded as they both instinctively turned away from the lights. Even when turned away neither could see for several seconds as the flash bulb memory held in their visual fields for up to ten seconds. The cyan light was green. Sabian continued. "The cyan lights were developed to cause massive discomfort to human eyes but with no lasting effects. They're also mains rechargeable which means there's no danger the batteries are going to suddenly die in the field, always the danger with a quartz battery watch. I've already synchronised them together." Sabian took a disappointing and disapproving glance at Brunner's watch. "They're water proof as well." Charlotte said "I don't like the colour, why all black metal?" Sabian answered without looking at her continuing to rummage around in the freight box. "They're black so your position is not given by sudden sunlight hitting a traditional stainless steel case. They're PVD coated as well so they shouldn't be any chipping." Charlotte sat with her chin resting on her hand looking at Sabian as if he were an obsessed man. "I'd like to say you don't get out much, but I simply know that is not true!" she said. Sabian glanced at her with passing interest and then continued sorting through the contents of the case. He threw two small black webbing bags to them. "In each of them you'll find a leather trouser belt with an internal security zip compartment. You'll find a myriad of goodies in them from cash to painkillers, handcuff keys and of course your standard cyanide pill. Only joking!. There's also a quick clot compound which can stop you bleeding to death and disposable face masks. They'll give you about twenty minutes breath time in a smoke environment, oh and there's a couple more space blankets in case you're out asleep under the stars again." Brunner was not paying attention; he was already trying on the designer sunglasses he had found in the bottom of his bag. He was turning his head from side to side totally blind in the blackness of the night. Charlotte swiftly dealt him a sharp dig to his left shoulder. "Owww!" He shouted out falling back into the sand. He started to laugh insanely still with the sunglasses firmly wrapped around his face staring into the black void. "I can see the dunes behind me" he managed to get out between fits of laughter. "There high-quality rear vision surveillance sunglasses" said Sabian. Brunner stopped laughing but with small cracks appearing at the corner of his mouth, his stomach muscles tensing a number of times trying to prevent a further eruption of insanity which he felt unable to control. The exhaustion and fear of the last couple of hours had drained him turning him into a giddy wreck. Sabian was still staring at Brunner with the passive look of an executioner and continued, "They also have three millimetres thick lens and can stop a thirty eight special bullet from fifteen yards." Brunner lost it again and laughed until he felt he could not breathe his stomach as tight as an ironing board cover.

"You've thought of everything haven't you Joe?" said Charlotte. Sabian had already threaded the belt around his middle and was slinking back into the cold still water. He raised the back of his hand toward Charlotte as he disappeared up to his chest. "See you both in the morning, stay here and stay low." In the next second he was gone like the slick hump of an Anaconda squirling over and under the waters surface.

Brunner spent five more minutes playing around with the lights on his watch trying to see if his sunglasses gave much protection to the flashbulb Cyan defence lights. He concluded that they did to a certain degree but still when he removed the glasses he was not able to see properly. Three strong light phantoms graced his field of vision as he strained to see and the unexpected vision of Charlotte who had stripped down to her bra and pants and was squeezing her soaking dress out at the waters edge. "Stop it with that watch." She said. "Someone will see us." Charlotte realising that Brunner was trying to survey her every curve, scurried back to her space blanket and pulled it up around her neck shivering and making a passing comment about the coldness. Brunner discarded some of his wet clothing and removing his sunglasses he pulled the aluminium sheet up close to his chin. She turned her face to him the darkness. "What's it like being a police-man?" "It has its moments!" Brunner said in a soft low voice. "You don't seem very enthusiastic." "It kind of gets knocked out of you. I spent a long time in uniform as a PC then as a sergeant. There were a lot of moments I was close to death, a lot of fear and tension that you feed of in the beginning but it can turn on you like a cancer. The greatest stress is generated not from the street or what you might encounter but from inside the job. The poor managers with their quotas and 'for strict compli-ance' orders. Many of them were there just to put a tick in the box for the next rank, to get some evidence for their next interview board. I'm not one of those people. Life's about more than putting ticks in boxes, it's about know-ing what paper your writing on and most important, what sort of ink are you using, a Sable or some cheap brand." Charlotte's eyes were becoming heavy as her own body heat encapsulated her in a cocoon of security. He did not notice. In time his eyes too became heavy and he slept. Charlotte rolled toward him; the two mirrored surfaces of the blankets touching each other.

Sabian swam for a solid twenty minutes in a straight line across the bay and up the slight dog leg stretch toward the Captains' Launch. On the jetty to the rear of the restaurant was the small white speedboat its outboard motor firmly at rest in a horizontal position. He was beginning to feel the physical excesses of the day and his stroke had become hesitant and laboured. Sabian concluded with his last two strokes that they had given up looking for them; at least on a water bound search. He felt sure that the Palm was no doubt the second port of call for the diplomatic sedan and Longinners' crew. Sabian suddenly imagined Longinner using his diplomatic status to put pressure on the night duty manager of the Palm to open up vacant rooms suspected to be theirs. A slip of money into the palm of a hand and the illicit searching that followed. Sabian used the outside flanks of the restaurants stilts to lift himself into the small boat after several minutes of treading water and half wanting to sleep. The boat bobbed and swayed with its new guest. Sabian turned on his back and despite the hardness of the skeleton of the hull putting pressure on his spine he felt comfortable. The restaurant was in darkness; the finger bowl candles long since extinguished. He stared up at the stars. The rhythm of movement generated by the boat quickly rocked him to sleep. There he slept for three hours.

With the sound of raised muffled voices he snapped his eye's open. He pulled the boat toward the stilts using both hands and reaching out. The boat tilted on its axis in the water for a split second and Sabian swivelled back to his previous position on his back fearing that it was about to capsize. Raising himself very gently he was able to see a French diplomatic flag fluttering on the top of the black sedan. Longinner's sharp heeled boots could be heard pacing the wooden floor of the restaurant. The voices; maybe two or three, definitely male remained muffled. Straining further Sabian could not improve his capacity to hear anymore. Soon the voices vanished completely with the dull thud of car doors and the screeching of tyres. Sabian again turned his head skyward and watching the stars for several more minutes could not cling to the conscious world any longer.

24

Blue Tiger Eye Signet Ring

As daylight was breaking he made his way along the wooded secluded path that followed the dusty road back into Grand Baie. Soon he came to an intersection where he stopped to study the upturned burned out remains of a Datsun Cherry. The sound of dawn was accompanied by the hoots of distant Peacocks and buzzing crickets in an orchestrated wall of noise. This had been the noise that had originally awakened him as he lay in the boat with increasing shivering bouts and pains along his battered spine.

He walked around the car several times looking at the road either side and up through the intersection that led to the Captains' Launch and beyond. He stopped feeling something hard under the thinnest part of sole on his shoe. Lifting his right foot he saw a piece of white metal partially covered by sand. He kicked the small object lightly displacing the sand around it. He saw an over-sized blue tiger eye signet ring flanked with much smaller white diamond like stones on either side of the blue stones setting. It was spattered with small flecks of blood. He recognised the design of the ring immediately as he leant and picked it up. It signified membership of the higher order of Ninja. The Ninjitsu were at the centre of the whole investigation into the Marimba Sphere manufacture. To some circles they were known as 'The Protectors' to others they were a cyclone of death of the most unimaginable and torturous design.

'The Protectors' operated with the most cunning, ingenious and creative stealth. They came and went like shadows on the sidewalk. They trained for years in the small sect holdings around the island. Sabian knew from briefings with Dacres that they were now a world wide organisation infiltrating covertly many political organisations. They made pots of money through extortion, money laundering and using their covert tactics to make money through exploits in industrial espionage.

Sabian turned the ring between his fingers, rusty flakes of blood spatter came away falling like rust particles leaving a light patina or redness on its shiny surface and between his fingers. The blue tiger eye stone sat proudly in the middle glinting in the rising sun. He slipped it into his trouser pocket and glancing back at the upturned Datsun a sickening feeling of realisation gripped his stomach.

25

Police ID

Brunner woke slowly as the sun broke through an opening in the trees. Charlotte was already awake with her back to him checking out the contents of the bag in the better light. The foil blanket sleeping bags had done their jobs well. Brunner had slept solidly and coldness had not disturbed him once, and in fact he felt too hot now as he started to tear the blanket off himself. Charlotte looked around startled by the sudden movement.

"How long have you been awake?" she asked.

"Just now, just woke, how about you?"

"Oh about twenty minutes, slept okay how about you?"

"Yeah fine, I could have slept on a razors edge after all that physical activity last night. I wonder when Joe will be back". Charlotte again glanced over her shoulder to see Peter standing about six to eight feet away with his back to her. He was urinating a thick yellow stream into the sand. "Could you not have done that a little further into those woods? Do you have no dignity?" Peter looked back at her without expression shaking himself and then walked to the shore edge where he rinsed both hands. "Didn't know it was that important to you after all that last night". Charlotte's face screwed up and she turned away from Peter who had just sat beside her. She folded her arms tight across her chest defensively. "You got a problem?" Peter enquired. "Nothing I can't handle thank you!" Peter lay back in the sand with his hands firmly pressed at the back of his head and stretching out closed his eyes. "You're not sleeping again are you?" she protested. "Have you got any better idea? We're supposed to wait here until Sabian gets back".

"And what if he doesn't come back. I'm beginning to think the man is quite insane. We don't know what he's capable of or what those he is so paranoid about are too!"

"Don't concern yourself too much. You need to get as much rest as possible. We don't know what we may have to confront later." Peter added as he rolled over facing away from her. "One thing you can do now before you sleep at least is do what you were told to yesterday and lose this!" Charlotte held in her hand his black leather police id wallet that had just fallen out of his back pocket. Peter turned and looking at it curiously snatched it lightly from her fingers. "I'll bury it in a minute."

Roger Folkestone and Camilla Dufus were both secret service field operatives and had been assigned to the Marimba project. Sabian had met neither of them but he had fleetingly glanced at their thin files when Dacres had left his office to speak to a HQ bigwig momentarily. He knew they had been working the project several weeks ahead of him and that Dacres would eventually get an encrypted message to him arranging a meet with the American counterparts when it was safe to do so. Sabian now feared this was not a realistic possibility anymore as he followed the blood spatters along the rocky path to the small hut in the clearing of the woods. As he got close to the door that was slightly ajar he had to use the bottom of his shirt as a makeshift filter for the stench. He noticed immediately the blood on the floor and against a far wall near an aluminium chute. As he turned to leave he saw a female arm from the elbow protruding from a large pile of manure. "Bastards! Bastards!"

26

Maurice Longinner

Maurice Longinner apart from being the main man in the Mauritian French Embassy had also for fifteen years been an avid and disciplined student to the eighteen disciplines of Ninjutsu. He had risen in that time to be the grand master of all the lodge holdings on the island. His particular strengths lay in his understanding and teachings of Bojutsu, stick and staff fighting. Of particular interest to Sabian and the intelligence services were his combined skills in Kayakujutsu, fire and explosives along with Choho, espionage and Boryaku, military strategy.

Longinner's large white Stetson sat finely balanced on top of the narrow locker as he reached inside and took the crisp white silk garments from their hangers. Once undressed, he slipped the loose fitting white top and leggings on along with the head covering leaving just a thin narrow letterbox opening where his two piercing blue eyes stared unblinkingly from. He briefly inspected the rim of the Stetson above him half imagining a fleck of dust. He removed from the upper shelf of the locker a rolling tape dust collector and just for good measure rolled it around the entire rim of the hat. He then neatly placed it back on top of the locker adjusting it several times so that its central point was squarely in the centre of the locker and facing due north. He then swiftly keyed in a five digit alpha numeric code into the small metal safe on the top shelf. With the sound of a small whine and the illumination of a red light he turned the handle and clicked the heavy door open. He removed from inside a small satin purple bag. He reached in again and removed a pair of white silk gloves. Stretching them onto each of his hands like a second skin he then removed from the purple bag a white metal heavy blue tiger eye signet ring. Placing it on the third finger of his right hand he adjusted its position a number of times admiring the way the bright fluorescent lights reflected the diamond filled shanks of precious metal.

He stood admiring himself in the full mirror adjacent to the locker. Returning to the locker he tied the single white cord around his waist and inserted a staff into the circular worn leather retainer. Just for good measure he removed it again and held it horizontally out between both hands in a concentrated fighting stance. Against the continuous flow of white washed walls behind him and the saturated fluorescent lighting he appeared almost invisible except for the cold steel of his ring with its blue stone that matched and reflected the stillness of his cruel staring eyes. Years of perfecting this, his true passion had past in the blink of an eye and now he stood on the precipice of total self indulgency of his art. He parried with his reflection making graceful swift moves with the staff. The nimbleness of his fingers had the practiced grace of a cheer leader. With a sudden flurry of movement the staff whistled and cut through the air and as if by sleight of hand was back in its belt retainer silent and still. He now stood like a statue, the black irises of his eyes, both small sharp razor like pin holes focused on the door leading to the fighting auditorium.

27

❧❧❧❧

The Auditorium

The Great Auditorium was a masterpiece of modern architectural design. Its high gothic arches of mahogany stretched some eighty feet where they touched each other at three separate apexes. As he entered a shaft of dusty light cut through the majestic gloom of the great hall as Longinner parried through onto the highly polished mahogany flooring. Whistles and snaps of air followed as his stick danced a macabre ritual in the half light. A single stained glass circular window graced each apex in the roof, each casting a combination of colourful hues down into the hall. Through a small clear leaded segment in the middle apex Sabian peered down uncomfortably and hanging on for all he was worth.

Sabian had spent the best part of fifteen minutes shimming up the highly grooved wooden and concrete outcrops that tailored their way to the top of the auditorium. He knew that this is where Longinner spent much of his spare time and he knew that the two American agents had been working deep cover within this establishment but in what capacity he was not entirely sure. The ring at the roadside which was now sticking into his groin as he adjusted his positioning had been a major clue. So had the Datsun. The blue stoned rings were only ever awarded to high ninjas. There were only ever a small number of them manufactured and he knew from the brief look at the agents files in Dacres office that Roger Folkestone had been given one as a prop for his mission in Mauritius. Sabian could not quite figure out how all this fitted together; but he knew that both the American agents were now dead and he wasn't, and he intended to remain that way.

Three great wooden doors were unexpectedly opened from their gothic recesses. In front of each opening stood a ninja; each in black combat uniform and each holding a staff. A gong sounded, its fury echoing inside the auditorium as all three ninja adopted a combatant ready stance. Longinner drew an imaginary semi circle with his staff in front of him about three inches above the highly polished flooring. He then touched the blue tiger eye stone of his signet ring six times in quick succession. His white silk covered fist gripped the fighting stick; his knuckles protruding and stretching the silk like the blanket covered mountains of the Alps. Without warning the three ninja moved like scurrying hornets from a stick poked nest. Longinner did not look at them. He stared at the blue stone of his ring his breathing deepening and his eyelids half open. Opponent number one from the north west aperture scuttled forward. The blow from his weapon was quick and sharp but was hastened by a high metallic sounding block from Longinners master arc. A second past; its stillness filled with the resonating of the two metal staffs vibrating microns from each others surface. The second seemed like a hundred years; an almost timeless expanse where the two figures stood themselves motionless. The merry joust then commenced; punctuated with moments of tormenting stillness followed by sudden rainfalls of violence. The resonating metal clanks became more frequent and the frozen stillness less frequent until there was just one wall of sound resonating through all the apexes of the great hall. The two other combatants that had been standing like mannequins then quickly joined the first. Sabian winced as a painful blow graced the two of them sending them through the air. Two more blows from the first opponent were counter blocked before the two felled hit the ground. Both lay motionless staring up at Sabian's position. He instinctively pulled himself from view thinking he had been rumbled, but when he glanced back he saw that the figures had not moved; both sets of eyes still staring up at the high gothic beams and pleasantly designed stain glass windows. The remaining ninja combatant shifted restlessly on the balls of his feet like a ballerina suddenly caught off guard by a break in the music caused by a scratch in a worthless recording. He took six paces backwards; bowing he placed his staff into his scabbard and shuffled backwards the twenty or so paces to his gothic retreat. The large wooden gothic arched door was opened and slammed shut without his intervention. Sabian mused at the idea that the doors must work on the principle of some pressure pad operation. Longinner grew impatient; the anger of his trance like state suddenly breaking to the surface. He ran toward the closed door, not like a highly skilled martial arts expert but as an insecure child who had had his toys taken away from him. He struck the door several times in wild and mounting violence. His body appeared to hang limp with resignation as he approached the two dead in the middle of the auditorium. He reached for each one of their hands in turn and removed a heavy gold ring with a large emerald. He could not remove the ring from the second adversary so he snapped the finger to make it all the more easy. Placing the two signet rings in a small opening just below his belt he vanished back into the dimly lit corridor leading to his changing room. A distant door slammed. The two black silken figures still looked up; a widening pool of blood filtered out from under them.

28

Where the Hell is Sabian?

Brunner placed his police identification wallet into a small resealable plastic bag and buried it in the sand near a small outcrop of distinctively identifiable ragged rock. From a certain angle the rock looked like the silhouette of a bust of Nelson Mandela. From other angles it looked like nothing at all. A fact which did concern him if he was going to locate this area again. Charlotte was busying herself getting dressed. Her black dress had dried out over night and all the creases had virtually dropped out. Brunner had watched as she pulled the garment over her hour glass figure. He felt like a perverted voyeur. A teenage boy lost in a wild fantasy! The peace was suddenly disturbed by the fast urgent approach of a motor boat. Both Peter and Charlotte dived instinctively for cover behind the small sand dune physically colliding with each other in the process. Nelson's craggy face looked down on Brunner; half Mandela half Elephant Man. The boat, a small two man fishing boat sped past without paying any attention to them, the island or Mandela for that matter. Brunner glanced at Mercedes. "When the hell is Sabian coming back?" he whispered through gritted teeth. "Give him time, give him time!"

"Any more time and I'm off across that bay with or without you. I guess there's no way on foot to the mainland from this place, I couldn't really tell last night in the dark?"

"No, you're right" said Charlotte. "Unless Sabian comes back with a boat we'll have to swim back."

"Oh wonderful. How long have you worked with Sabian?" he asked.

"A few months, still can't figure him out much though."

"Have you made contact with the American agents yet?"

"No, we we're meant to meet them in two nights time at the Captains' Launch. I guess that's kind of out the question now!"

Peter turned and looked at Charlotte again, their faces hovering several inches from each other. Brunner suddenly moved closer trying to kiss her but Charlotte turned away and he hesitated, his lips hovering over her cheek. He moved from her slowly at first and then threw himself onto his back in the sand. Staring at the clear blue sky he felt rejected and foolish and just a tiny bit sad. "Sorry!" he managed to get out. His pride cut in two.

"No need to be."

29

Stetson

Sabian waited and waited for the big man to emerge from the changing room at the back of the auditorium. He finally emerged his cream cowboy boots gleaming in the sun, his white Stetson on his head half cocked over his left eye. Longinner made his way to another building some hundred or so feet away. His pace was hastened by his hat being suddenly torn from his head with the wind stream of his fast progression. The hat somersaulted half a dozen times over the sand dust and rocks. Longinner's eyes filled with horror as he hurriedly collected the obscene item from the ground. Inspecting it with both hands from every angle he growled and crushed it with both hands and threw it to the ground like a discarded ball of tissue. Sabian watched from a small veranda he had climbed down to. It was a much more welcome place to be. Sabian noticed the small sand storm approach caused by the black funeral parlour van. It stopped very close to the auditorium and just below the veranda. He watched studiously as two suited and booted men entered the auditorium emerging several minutes later with two dead weights being dragged along in body bags. The black van with its unexpected cargo then made off in a cyclone of sand and dust up the ever narrowing road and out of sight. Once the coast was clear he climbed over the low veranda and hung over the side allowing himself to drop the four to five feet still below him. Using some of the line of the buildings as cover he made his way in the same direction that Longinner had just taken.

Once at the other building he noticed that the door Longinner had entered had not been closed properly. It gaped open by about two inches. He could see only blackness beyond. He felt an increasing desire to just rush in but instead listened hard for any internal noises. This was difficult due to the raised singing of the crickets from the wooded area to the side of the land that encompassed the auditorium and its small estate of out buildings. The other buildings appeared bland and without structure in comparison to the great lodge of the gothic auditorium. Sabian creaked the door open another inch and peered into the darkness. There were no obvious signs of life so he entered. It was impossible to see anything inside so he ignited the lights on his Ingersoll and saw that he was in a narrow corridor with an open staircase above him. He crept up the stairs; his silhouette danced a ghostly ritual on the white washed plastered walls as the lights from his wrist moved with his arm along the rail. As he approached the final flight of stairs he stopped at the slightest sound of voices from a distant room. He extended his arm along the rail lowering his body position in an attempt to exploit the sound source. The twisting deformed stretching arm of Nosferatu mirrored his movement on the wall.

30

Ninja Spiders

Mysterious stealth like movement was taking place only twenty feet away from where Charlotte and Peter lay. Six pairs of eyes darted and blinked from letterbox openings in head coverings. The six ninja moved through the wooded area without noise. Not a single branch or twig faltered under their guile and approach.

Two of them had acted as a forward reception for the others hanging like vampire bats from two medium sized oak branches the best part of an hour. Still and motionless, their black silk garb fluttering in the breeze that periodically danced its way through the trees from across the bay. Their split toe canvass boots hung over the branches. They looked like the feet of the dodo, long since extinct from this island paradise. Years of practiced meditation of controlling muscle and fine motor nerves allowed the insides of their feet to clasp the branch like limpets. Two short Boju warrior staffs protruded below their heads like sore fingers pointing straight down to hell; or the upturned periscopes of hapless submarines.

They had arrived under cover of darkness and awaited the sunrise. When finally it arrived with a low burst of redness reflected in their now still and bloodshot glassy eyes they still did not stir. As the dawn graced itself over the marina bay four more black garbed ninja moved like an army of black widow spiders through the undergrowth toward Brunner and Mercedes and the hanging bats. Each moved with the terrifying unnerve that only the fast unexpected scurry of a spider can instil. Stealthily and relentlessly over all obstacles in their path, with total consuming interest in the prey. Once the four spiders saw the bats they stopped, limbs eyes and senses motionless. Like a scurrying arachnid that suddenly stops when aware of your presence in a room with maybe a singularly hairy black leg hovering in the air; an antenna picking up small eddies of air and droplets of perspiration; feeding off the currents of impending danger. The two bat like ninja did not need to look. Their senses too were highly developed. They felt the presence of reinforcements; a sense of being stared at.

Each bat ninja in unison removed from their utility belt pouches a finely pointed stainless surgical steel dart. Flightless; each had a small bluish tinge to its tip. Each dart was about the size of a match. With uniform and mirrored precision the darts were placed onto the tongue of the ninja through small slits in their head coverings. Timing was everything. The powerful poison could paralyze and kill a ninja if not used in an ancient and skilled fashion. Either swallowing or allowing the dart to stay on the wet surface of the tongue for more than three seconds could be fatal. For this reason they had been breathing through their mouths for over an hour and not allowing any saliva build up. Their tongues were dry and starting to appear cracked as the missiles were loaded into their sandpaper crevices. Well defined and trained muscles in the tongue and throat jettisoned each torpedo through an almost microscopic opening from each set of pursed lips with a continuous and furious stream of air.

Brunner was struck by a dart in his left shoulder and Mercedes in the small fleshy base of her back. Neither had time to respond. They both hit the sand at precisely the same time. The four spider ninja scurried past the hanging bats and quickly bound the two unconscious and paralyzed victims.

Once blindfolded and gagged the two bats dropped to earth with the flourish of somersaults, each landing with a synchronised thud. The first real sounds to be made by any of them. One of them quickly unearthed the self seal plastic bag and its contents that Brunner had only buried a minute or two before. The ninja did not check the contents placing it into a black canvass bag attached to his belt.

The ninja then removed from the bag a small match-box sized orange container and gingerly placed the two used darts into it snapping it shut. Even modern day ninja carried sharps containers. The small fishing boat that Peter and Charlotte had earlier been quick to dismiss glided almost soundlessly from around the corner crewed by two ninja with squat black paddle like implements. Peter and Charlotte were loaded onto the boat. The six ninja vanished into the blackness of the woods. The two in the boat gave a gentle tug to their costumes which came away like the scales of butterfly wings to reveal sedate tourist clothing underneath. One of them quickly lifted an already floated and flied fishing rod and cast it from the boat whistling to himself, as the other placed a baseball cap on his head and pulled the rip cord on the outboard motor. Brunner and Mercedes were en route like prize catches in the bottom of the boat uncomfortably being taken back in the direction of the Captain's Launch.

Sabian continued to move cautiously up the last flight of stairs. He could hear the distant sound of activity, like automated factory noise, hissing pistons, gears and hydraulics. Every few seconds there was a long low horn sound. These came at random intervals. Sabian was sure that it was not an alarm for him and his entry to the complex. To remain absolutely certain he tucked himself into a small recessed area under the last flight of stairs and closing the door on himself set his watch for a twenty minute countdown to assess any possible activity before he decided to make his next move.

31

Tattooist's Needles

Peter's eye lids were heavy like lead. He tried to open them but they hammered shut without reason. He could hear the sound of water running and a creaking and straining noise. He felt vaguely sea sick, like he was moving or spinning. There were low muffled indistinguishable voices all around him.

Charlotte was the first to scream. Sabian's ears pricked up at the distant sound of the scream. He slinked back into the dark turret of the staircase and the sound of the scream echoed from several flights below. The Ingersolls lights came on indicating his twenty minute wait was up. 'Charlotte' lit up like a neon sign in his head. As he sprinted down the stairs he was cursing to himself with anger at the idea that they had been foolish enough to allow themselves to be caught; by god knows what means and by whom. The Ingersolls LEDs darted like ghostly fire flies on his face, leaving their heat signature streaks through the darkness as he heaved to catch his breath in the dusty sticky environment. He could hear Longinner's voice booming, its timbre and pitch were an exact match. He could not decipher the words which only added to his deepening despair and frustration.

Inside the dimly lit room with its battleship grey walls both Peter and Charlotte were bound to chairs. Bindings several strands strong wrapped themselves around their ankles and wrists. Around each of their waists were thick black leather belts securing them steadfast to the back of the chairs. Each chair had no seat area allowing their backsides to sink several inches into the body of the cheap wicker designs. The two chairs span wildly; each suspended by a single poorly made frayed hemp rope binding attached to the back of them. They were suspended at forty five degrees in their helpless states. The room was spinning like a cyclone. Alvin and Flagg were laughing insanely and Maurice Longinner now stood silently, a new Stetson gracing the top of his head. The place smelt damp and dark like a sewer. Below each chair were a series of sharpened bamboo stakes, three feet below the swirling victims. Four stakes below each victim, each stake about four feet long and cemented into old whisky barrels. Double distilled for you drinking pleasure each barrel announced in large faded black lettering. Water dropped from two openings in the ceiling just about the same place where the top of the rope bindings ended, hooked over two rusty butcher hooks. Green mould covered the hooks and fresh white mould was already forming a stalagmite formation where each hook was firmly secured by an industrial strength bolt into the reinforced steel girders. Small droplets of dirty foul smelling water trickled down the dense fibres and weave of each creaking binding as they flexed with the spinning of the pendulums below them.

"Release us you bastards!" Brunner protested as the three faces flashed by for about the five hundredth time. Flagg quickly drew a seven inch hand sharpened blade from the scabbard on his belt and held it three inches from the binding securing Brunner's chair.

"You want me to release you. Do you? Who is the bastard now?" With that he jerked the blade forward allowing it to caress the binding. Several sinewy strands popped under the strain and the keenness of his blade.

"Stop!" Protested Longinner stepping forward and raising his big right palm up to Flagg's grinning features. A deadly silence ensued filling the room with expectation. Longinner's spurred boots echoed in the room as he took several steps toward Brunner. The metallic clinking echoed as an after thought from the impact of his boots on the slightly raised walling that separated him from the water that gathered below the whisky barrels. Sabian stood in the darkest recess of the room pressing his back hard against the cold damp concrete and trying to exert all control over his breathing and the frantic rhythm of his drumming heart beat. He did not dare move. Flagg was an insane unknown quantity in the room. One wrong move from Sabian and Flagg would not take much to disobey his boss, Longinner. Flagg's blood lust was already up. Longinner's voice cold and in control broke the silence that was periodically broken by the sound of the stressing and straining bindings.

"At last we all meet. Charlotte Mercedes and Peter Brunner I believe. How nice to meet both your acquaintance!" Longinner opened a black leather wallet he had been concealing in the palm of his right hand and scanning its contents spoke with a pleasant grimace cracking the corners of his mouth. "And New Scotland Yard, we are indeed honoured. Are we not gentlemen?" He posed the statement as just that and not a question. Flagg's eyes darted toward Longinner and back to his blade that he now held by his side. His lips were still drawn back over his gleaming white teeth and pink gums. Alvin was shifting back and forth on the balls of his feet looking impatiently and fearfully between Flagg and Longinner. "Lets just do them boss!" Neither looked at or acknowledged Alvin. Longinner continued, "As my guests of honour this fine morning you will be happy to know that you are both about to be subjected to an ancient ninjitsu ritual of torture which I have been lead to believe by the good Mister Flagg has been highly effective in the past." He glanced at Flagg who threw his head back laughing. Longinner's eyes cut him off with a disapproving flash of their whites. "Just give me the nod and Mister Flagg will despatch you and release you from this life quick and easily. Your bindings will be cut and you will free fall several feet onto the stakes below. Death will be fairly instantaneous. The stakes are guaranteed to pierce both your hearts within the second it takes them to travel the full length of your intestines and spleen via your rectums. I will also order your despatch if you give me some answers."

"Why should we cooperate?" Charlotte spat. "Why cooperate under these terms of condition?"

"Because my darling Mercedes, if you do not I will leave you both in this room where the slow dripping water down the vines that hold you will cause them over a period of hours, perhaps up to a day to elongate and stretch to the point where you will feel the spikes caressing your perfectly formed buttocks. Now you may think that by shifting your body weight in those contraptions that you can avoid the piercing of your marble like flesh, - and I'm sure in the beginning you will achieve the level of success you desire, rest assured as time ticks by fatigue and disorientation will engulf you and the stakes will penetrate very very slowly until the tips burst your labouring hearts, puncturing them into stillness forever in a catastrophic burst of beauty. Many have tried and equal amounts have failed to escape this ancient art. I suppose it's like your ancient ritual for dealing with witches on a ducking stool. If you did not drown you were burnt at the stake for being a witch. So what shall it be? Quick or slow? Your choice sports fans! Tell me where is Mister Sabian?" Sabian tried to push himself further into the recess that had no more space and that he knew would take no more of his physical form. He remained confident that for the time being at least he could not be seen.

Brunner was feeling extremely sea sick and his stomach heaved a couple of times but he was still able to exert dwaning physical control over his faculties as Flagg's terrifying macabre grin flashed by on the merry ground ride from hell.

"We're not going to tell you anything, what would be the point? And who the fuck are you anyway?" shouted Brunner. Longinner removed his Stetson revealing his greying blond thick main of hair and piercing blue cold eyes.

"You do not recognise me Mister Brunner. How very sad and uninspiring indeed."

He looked at Flagg. "Hold his chair for me." He stepped forward and grabbed the spinning chair as Longinner took a step or two forward so that his features became clearer to Brunner. Peter's head felt too heavy for his shoulders and it lolled from side to side to side the giddiness and sickness worse than ever. Longinner's face slowly pulled into focus. "I am Maurice Longinner

Mister Brunner, the Attaché to the French Embassy in Mauritius. You must have been briefed and at least shown a photograph of me before your arrival in this paradise? We were meant to meet with your pals at the Captains Launch. But alas these plans had to be cut short somewhat due to unforeseen circumstances. Unforeseen intervention from your bigger friends from the United States of Anxiety. You're here because of the all important Marimba Spheres. I was meant to help you but I was made a much better offer you see. I can tell you this because of that offer and it doesn't matter that I tell you. You'll not be in a position to tell anyone else. I have a new boss now. She has paid me handsomely and more riches are on there way. You see the Spheres that your governments have been so keen to chase for so long are just prototypes, deadly prototypes I give you that. Show him Alvin." Alvin who was stood closer to Longinner than Flagg leant down beside the big man and opening a small black dirty canvass bag from a recess took out a crystal skull. Its jaw mandibles and eye sockets moulded to perfection. The structure was seamless and without design fault. Inside was a red viscous gel substance that swirled in a small slow motion vortex of lava. Alvin held the skull out at arms length. Light bounced off its crystal structure bouncing rainbow prismic designs, random and fleeting against the grey walls. Longinner continued, "Don't worry; this is just an inert model. It is hair gel inside, but the real crystal skulls will have the power to destroy substantial infrastructure causing massive collateral damage and loss of life. Our factories are about to start production very shortly. Once the first batch is produced here in Mauritius the plans will be sent worldwide to our eager and awaiting cells so that their destructive power can be felt worldwide. It's all in the mix you see, a new and soon to be improved chemical formula". Brunner stared at the crystal skull coldly and without expression. Longinner took the skull from Alvin and caressed the curve of its forehead and held it at arms length as if to deliver some eloquent speech. "How beautiful and perfect it is, wouldn't you agree Mister Brunner? How about you Miss Mercedes?" Charlottes chair see sawed and she appeared semi-conscious as Brunner stared wildly with disbelief at Longinner a mad man and his novel piece of bizarre technology. Sabian remained still as a statue. Beads of perspiration running down his cheeks and like small centipedes down his back. He could use the Beretta but he'd already completed a brief risk assessment of the damage limitation in his head. He didn't know if they all had firearms. Maybe one or two, maybe just Longinner, maybe all three. Flagg clearly had a knife that he was more than capable and willing to use. He alone could do more than massive damage to either Brunner or Mercedes even with a clear shot from this distance. Sabian remembered from a training session that an opponent with a knife can clear up to twenty five feet against an adversary in the process of drawing a gun. Flagg himself was only three to four feet away from the straining vines that held Peter and Charlotte. One line he remembered well from his training was 'is that they're only two forms of risk, high and unknown and that each situation should be approached with that in mind if nothing else. He remained still, his Beretta in the firm leather recess of an ankle holster.

Charlotte's mind was spinning, what was left of it. Her hair was lank and wet as water trickled down the side of her face and over the swell of her left breast. The water was dirty and had brown streaks in it. Through the mud of her mind she carelessly wondered if her Tetanus injections were up to date. Longinner still held the crystal skull. "She designed them you know, the Lady, the boss, these skulls of doom. She spoke to me; spoke to all of us at great length about them, the whys and wherefores, although I've never met her in person. I would like to one day. Perhaps we will be lovers. Let me give you both a bit of a history lesson of the legend of the crystal skulls. Real crystal skulls are very rare, possibly only half a dozen in the whole world. Some say that they weren't made by man at all, but were crafted and left by aliens as communication devices that will burst into life with some grand telepathic message for all mankind when the circumstances are right; perhaps when the stars are aligned in a certain way. Some sacred geometry awaits us all and their arrival we are told. I must confess I don't fully understand it all. Others say that the real skulls were made by generations of families, crafted by hand using only the pressure of generations of smoothing hands and water, rubbing for centuries the hard quartz. How absolutely incredible and wouldn't you say it's a strange coincidence that all our modern communication technology is based on quartz as its main component?" He paused seemingly savouring the moment, pondering his new position in the cosmos of his own making. Then thrusting the skull back toward Alvin he placed the Stetson back on his head. Alvin took it and placed it carefully into his black bag as if it could be as volatile as the real thing. Flagg was becoming impatient with the history lesson and had removed from his back pocket a leather sharpener on which he slowly and deliberately moved the blade of his knife back and forth on. The soft scraping was accompanied by the creaking vines that had become tighter and tighter, the sinews drawing together the wetter they became. Brunner had already moved six inches closer to the tips of the stakes below. Charlotte had moved about four inches closer. Brunner looked up at the straining vine, now wrecked by Flagg's blade. Half a dozen splayed strands neatly cut sprouted like fibre optics from the vine. Longinner continued "You will not stop the bombings!" Charlotte then spoke, "You can do all you like to us; others will come in our place. You don't think it's just us involved, do you? You would have to be totally naïve to believe that. Your numbers will come up eventually. Even after we're dead!"

"I do believe you maybe correct Miss Mercedes, but you will never know that will you. You will never have that pleasure! So just tell me where is Mister Sabian?" Flagg stopped his soft scraping of his blade and the vines creaked and groaned. "I could leave you here in the company of Mister Flagg. I'm sure he will find things to amuse you with. I've already seen the result of his handiwork in the last twenty four hours."

"Leave them with me boss, we'll have ourselves a mighty fine party!" Longinner again cut Flagg with a glance and Flagg grimaced. He would like to kill the big man if he could. Only if he had that final push of determination and motivation at the end of his desire. But even Flagg was not that stupid and ignorant. He knew Longinner was a powerful man who was well connected, and that there would be no escape from his army of darkness lurking in the recesses of the island that would fall on him like a dark cloak whilst he slept or went about his normal everyday life. He chose in the end as always to do nothing! But wait!

32

Diemetriana

The shimmering azure waters of the nearby bay reflected like a mirror, a savannah of tropical palms swaying gently in the mid morning breeze. Like a holiday post-card of a tropical idyll; a sharp contrast and juxta position to the activity taking place in a white stilted building less than two hundred yards away. Sun bathers had already gathered in swathes and expensive speedboats were lowered down concrete ramps into the clear blue stillness. People walked along wooden jetties towards moored yachts; whilst some emerged for the start of a new day, bright hopeful and full of expectation. A local with a blue baseball cap turned backwards with 'ESSO' emblazoned on it in red cast a fishing line into the bays water from a makeshift homemade fishing rod. A small transistor radio at his feet at low volume trickled out a hurried cackle of lightly tapping conga drums. The Diemetriana, a black and white speed boat was uncou-pled from a trailers shackles and chains, the four by four Discovery wheels spinning unintentionally away up the slightly inclined concrete landing area. The boats outboard motors were kicked over and its water pumps farted, gurgling and pumping several geezers of water.

The man with the ESSO baseball cap suddenly and unexpectedly felt a strain on his rod as it became heavy between his hands. His first catch of the day.

Nearby on a piece of disused and derelict land behind an electrified fence in the woods a white out building on stilts of concrete held the real first catch of the day. Its dark wooden shutters held the two realities of different worlds firmly apart. Two dead and decaying cars sat like decomposing animals in the clearing below the shuttered building. The cars sat at forty five degrees to each other in the sand, dust and dried vegetation. An old Ford Consul without windows and a Mercedes, diplomatic class that once belonged to Longinner. A car that had served him well until a fatal shooting inside left a smell in there that he could no longer tolerate in the tropical heat. The registration plate read BAD666.

Another fifteen minutes past and Sabian continued to cling in the dark recess of the room. The vines had lowered another seven inches. Charlotte's eyes were heavy as she drifted in a world of demented and resigned oblivion. Brunner felt pretty much the same. The last twenty four hours had been the worst in his life.

33

Droplets of Spittle

"Where is Sabian? I am tiring of this now, where is he?" shouted Longinner. Brunner spat in his direction. A large globule of flem and spittle struck the ridge of his Stetson like a paintball exploding on a solid target. Longinner's eyes opened, doubling their size yet the pupils constricting into two small pin holes. He removed the offending article from his head which he had just that morning purchased from the islands exclusive 'Monique Boutique' as a replacement. He looked insanely at the dripping mucus stain and toward Flagg and Alvin. "You've got fifteen minutes, use them well." Longinner tossed the Stetson at Brunner. It span briefly through the air like a death star spur glancing his cheek and flicking droplets of his own spittle over his face and shoulders. Longinner turned his back on the two suspended chairs and paced away, his spurs clinking as he vanished through a door that when opened kissed the room with the liquid gold of the sun. Brunner turned away from the searing light. The room was then snapped back into darkness, but not before Brunner saw Sabian's expressionless face in the high aperture of the room. Sabian had flinched initially as the door had been opened, moving his naked face back from the light like a vampire trying to evade the rising sun. Brunner had felt extreme fear and apprehension along with a low thud in his guts. He felt a singularly desperate need to say Sabian's name and to demand to know where he had been. Flagg and Alvin with their backs to Sabian had not seen him. They were both staring at Charlotte who was to all intents and purpose unconscious. Flagg had a rising explosion of lust in his face and a growing erection in his shorts.

The strong expensive luxury black and white hull of the Diemetriana slowly caressed the blue crystal clear water as the two middle aged men pushed it clear of the mooring pinions and thick rusty retainer chains that ran the full course of the marina ramp. The two men were heavily tanned and spoke quick short bursts of French. Both were in their fifties and sporting light cotton short sleeved shirts, one plain twill, the other a subtle Hawaiian design, crisp and clean. The one with the plain shirt had a particularly heavy stainless steel Rolex Submariner. The one with the green bezel insert. People have money around these parts. Once the boat was some fifteen feet into the water and clear of the ramp both men boarded pulling themselves from the shallow embrace of the water. They rummaged through a dusty box of reels rods and tackle. The man with the expensive watch took a momentarily fleeting and admiring glance at his timepiece not even noticing the time as it glinted a ray of sunshine just as he pressed the green ignition button. A single dim green light declared ignition and the soft burr of the concealed propeller blades needed the liquid around them and the Diemetriana was propelled forward. A school of fish darted and weaved for cover their spines a kaleidoscope of colour. An explosion in a paint factory. A small light shelled crab vanished under a plume of sand that span in a mini vortex, then it was gone drawing the fine powder into a flat flawless false horizon above its small fragile form. The cyclone and thunder of swirling water ravaged the environment, as the Diemetrianas blades stepped up a gear tearing through the water for purchase. Thrusting itself forward a white trail of froth and bubbles remained in its wake, reeds swaying in a gentle underwater breeze. The small crabs claw lifted partially the particles around itself, pausing for a brief second before pulling itself up onto the sand bed where it scurried off sideways into a dark recess of rocks at the edge of the mooring ramp.

34

Steady on Dear Chap!

Flagg walked deliberately toward Charlotte tapping the steel battered blade of his knife against his shorts. There was no emotion in his face. Alvin took a step back as if to try and hide further back into the gloom of the pit. Sabian knew he would have to act soon. He felt his hand slowly reaching down his right leg toward the Beretta almost as if part of him had made the decision already. It was like he was watching himself with some deep primitive auto pilot taking over. Brunner was staring toward the darkened recess where he had seen Sabian's features, as Flagg started to cut through the thin Lycra dress near the hem of Charlotte's shaking and goose pimpled body. Water was now running in rivers along the vines that held them both. The base of the room was drenched with filthy brown water as it slowly dissipated away to a swirling plug hole at one inclined piece of the concrete flooring. Sabian could feel the trusty reliable grip of his gun at the end of his fingers and the well worn brown leather holster. He knew to reach any further forward would put his upper torso and face within the semi lit area of the room and betraying his presence. He was just contemplating this when he felt the smooth edge of a ninja baton lifting his chin to its original position and the click of a gun in the darkness. Brunner's eyes were widening in horror and hopeless apprehension and Charlotte moaned in her semi-conscious state. Flagg turned around; carelessly his knife cut a layer of skin on Charlotte's left thigh, but not enough to cause bleeding. A ninja dressed in black stood in the flickering recess as Sabian was edged out of his retreat with a small black handgun held at his throat with his chin raised still by the baton so he stared at the ceiling. With the flick of a switch two flickering fluorescent strip lights filled the gloom of the room as two more ninja stepped out from other darkened areas of the room and into the arrhythmic strobe like effect of the lights. Charlotte's eyes opened a crack and she let out a short sharp scream as Brunner's chair suddenly dropped about six more inches as his ruptured vine started to untangle itself. He closed his eyes a lump rising quickly into his throat and a thumping in the pit of his stomach that echoed along to his swollen and constricted wrists and ankles. Sabian went instinctively to move forward as the barrel of the pistol was thrust against his left temple. The circular metal of the barrel made a dull noise as it struck bone sending a neuralgic sensation down the side of his face to his jaw which made him wince. The pain was incredible but he did not move again. He did not want half his face blown away. He was ushered down from the platform and moved closer to the centre of the room where another chair was lowered with a jolting motion from the ceiling. Flagg moved impatiently toward Sabian. "You are him, - Joseph Sabian! Strange I expected someone much bigger and capable. You are just a weak ant and I intend to crush you!" Sabian did not respond. The ninja baton still held his jaw shut and now pushed him with a bit more vigour toward the new chair. "Steady on dear chap!" Sabian managed to get out. The other ninja in the room stood like shop mannequins. Sabian was pushed into the seat. Two ninja rushed forward and using vine bindings for his feet and wrists secured him to the chair where he was slowly raised six feet above the ground; suspended like the others at an uncomfortable forty five degrees. A dirty stream of water immediately ran the full length of the single taught vine that held the chair that now slowly span on its own momentum. Flagg started to push the barrel of spikes that was under Charlottes chair under Sabians. Charlotte's eyes were heavily opened and with a slow drawl she said "Joe what are we to do?"

"Don't ask me dear girl, I just work here!" he spat out insensitively. Sabian suddenly felt last nights Bourbon hit his throat as if he were drinking the damn stuff again except this time it smarted like half a dozen razor blades had been rammed to the back of his tongue. The ninja had become statue like again and had withdrawn into darker parts of the room as Flagg took the thick shimmering blade from his scabbard again and tossed it from hand to hand, jabbering to himself under his breath. He turned suddenly and lashed out with the blade wildly toward Charlotte whilst transfixed on Sabian whose chair had stilled itself. Charlotte screamed. The tip of his blade struck the back of the chair and caused it to spin. Flagg tossed his head back laughing as only the insane can.

The Diemetriana was now about two hundred yards into the bay. The man with the expensive watch was moving the rod to and fro as it buckled and bent under a great strain. The other man cut the power to the boats engines and came to his aid. Both fought with the rubber grip of the rod and eventually with the combined strength of both of them placed the handle into the securing metal barrel where it locked with a precision click.

As Charlottes chair was spinning Flagg again thrust the blade toward her vine. Its nicked sinews splayed on contact. Twisting and splaying it snapped like the delicate leg of a dragon fly. The force of the chair hitting the ground snapped both its back legs but not before the jolt shook Charlotte's spine and base of her skull like a dozen jack hammers. A number of weak capillaries in her right nostril exploded causing a thick stream of bright red bubbly blood to spatter forth just before the chair fell backwards. Flagg turned to Brunner's vine and using his free hand span the chair so that it turned like a carousel. Flagg then flashed out blindly and deliberately towards his vine. The only thing that remained fixed within Brunner's vision was the barrel and its deadly array of spikes. "Jesssuuuss!" He screamed. "Go suck your mamma!" Flagg sneered between fits of laughter. Turning to Sabian he held his chair steadfast and hastily placed the blade against Sabian's muscled yet weak and fragile throat. It chaffed and dragged at his flesh just above his jugular. Sabian stared passively at Flagg, every flicker of emotion hidden. He did not want to give him the satisfaction.

"Mister Sabian we will have some fun later. That's of course if the vine has held out long enough. I will weaken it for you and turn the water flow up. Nice up the party a bit more." Flagg then moved to a darkened area and turned a rusty creaking tap. A pump could be heard and the water gushed down Sabian and Brunner's vines. Sabian's wet hair hung limply over his eyes, fast discoloured rivulets of water spawning a network of channels across his forehead, cheekbones and onto his shirt, its cotton weave becoming dense and heavy with the resulting wetness. From mid blue to dark blue it changed as the dark phantom of water stain reached out toward his waistline. Turning back to the vine Flagg lightly dragged the blade across the sinews, splaying several. He took the blade away and with a cock of his head to the side returned the blade and splayed several more cutting through about a quarter of the vines total depth.

"You sick bastard!" Brunner shouted. Flagg did not respond. He moved to the back of Charlottes' fallen chair grabbing the wooden slab of the back rest and began dragging it along the concrete floor. Its uneven surface jolted and jarred through Charlotte who stirred and began to shake her head, blood drying in a thick brown cracked network over her lower face and chest. Her hands and lower arms still bound to the back of the chair were a sea of cuts and bruises as they scraped along the hard surface of the floor under her full weight. Flagg and Charlotte vanished through the opening that Longinner had vanished into earlier. Light filled the room but all the ninja were gone.

The man with the expensive watch quickly and efficiently gutted the medium sized catch and threw the still twitching carcass of the fish into a large red icebox. Throwing a few handfuls of ice over the thing he closed the lid entombing it in darkness forever!

35

Lycra Dress

When Charlotte opened her eyes she was in a much smaller yet still darkened room. There was a smell of urine and sweat. A single dirt covered and smeared low wattage bulb sat in the middle of the ceiling kicking out what light it could. A bluebottle danced an arc around the thing. Her hands and arms hurt like hell and she was still on her back attached to the wooden chair, her full body weight on her arms. Flagg's grinning features suddenly engulfed her field of vision like an obscene apparition. Flagg cut and ripped the thin paper like dress off her in an almost single furious movement. She scanned the room hoping to see ninja, anyone or anything that would abate the look of sheer psychopathic lust in the madmans eyes. Did they possess some kind of magic that could make themselves transform from one place to another. Flagg had vanished to the side of the room and her pain did not allow her to turn and see what he was doing. Then there was silence and she wondered if he had left or had died of some physical weakness. Oh god how she wanted him dead. She lay there for what seemed like hours but was probably only minutes. Her pains had become numb sensations that only burned with their fire when she tried to move. Even an inch. Her mind turned toward the pure horror of her plight and that of Joseph and Peter. Were they still alive? She did not know. She could hear nothing except the damn fly that was now paying a particular interest in her and with growing annoyance made several passes over her blood caked face as she tossed her head from side to side spitting at it. The fly swooped across her taut stomach and twisting her body the fly was airborne again like a Harrier Jump Jet. The movement had restored some welcome circulation into her hands and arms. Pain came back quickly in thick pulses and she lay exhausted by the routine. Her heart was pounding in her ear drums, a double beat and a forced gush. Her eye lids were heavy. Her mind fought against the temptation to sleep. She did not want to enter the blackness forever, and certainly not as a willing participant and volunteer. She thought of as a child how she would holiday regularly at Mackenzie Beach in Larnaca, Cyprus and how the lazy summers stretched forever. She saw herself as an eight year old sitting on the beach. The hot sun beating a pleasant dance onto her sandy limbs as her father handed her an ice cream. The ice cream ran rivulets over his weather beaten labourers' knuckles and wrists, her father who had been dead for the last four years. What a beautiful smile he had, a smile like Peter Brunner's. Her eyes snapped open again and the Larnaca beach tumbled from her grasp. She loved her father and missed him terribly but she was not yet ready to meet him in the darkness, was not ready to take the step over the threshold separating what felt was left of her life and whatever lay beyond. The stark pain hit her body like a thunderbolt and the sound of her own breathing suddenly filled the room, deeper and deeper, faster and faster. My god I'm hyperventilating must keep calm, keep calm. She hadn't had an asthma attack since; since; Larnaca beach suddenly filled her head again, the ice cream tossed into the sand and her father's big strong arms cradling her, "She's gone again Lizzy, where's the god damn inhaler?"

The door burst open and Daemon Flagg stood like a gunslinger, his blade still in his hand and a can of extra strong lager in the other. He gulped down the last dregs and crushing the can tossed it with a flourish to the ground. He stepped into the room dragging the blade along the rough concrete wall. A shower of sparks exploded from the blades tip.

"I want me some meat, some woman meat!" The door closed with a terminal thud.

The Diemetriana was loaded onto the back of the trailer. The man with the Rolex opened the cool box to check the half a dozen fish that had been caught on the trip. Their gutted staring bodies stared up at him as he rubbed salt into their thick shinning silver skins. He smiled and snapped the lid shut.

Charlottes breathing became still almost at once. With the slamming of the door her throat passage opened. She took a single deep invigorating breath and then breathed normally watching the dark phantom above her. Flagg leant forward so his face was nearly touching hers. There was a smell of stale alcohol and bad halitosis. Putting his tongue out he lightly traced the contour of her face without touching it down from her forehead over her nose and lips and lightly touching her chin. The metallic saltiness of her dried blood invaded his senses. He rolled his thick pink tongue over his lips and his eyes flashed flickering back into their sockets.

She tried to move her head further back from him but it was already buried against the hard unyielding concrete. He continued to trace his tongue along the line of her throat, the beating jugular elevating the taste to its tip. Arriving at the soft heaving mound of a breast he pulled back the bra and took a full lustful mouthful of her nipple and a large portion of her upper breast, sucking hard. She squirmed and tried to tense away but it was fruitless. "Fuck off, fuck off you bastard!" She followed this by a scream that punctured the labyrinth of dark damp corridors and into the room where Sabian and Brunner hung helplessly. Brunner was exhausted with the spinning and Sabian could feel the graze of the top of a bamboo spike touching his left buttock. He tried to spin himself out of its line of attack but it lightly graced his flesh again through his thin trousers like a tattooist's needle. His vine was now making infernal straining noises that he feared marked the end of the sell by date. Brunner was shivering and soaked in water. His teeth chattered uncontrollably. "Sabian we've had it!" Sabian did not answer. The spike was starting to cause a small rip in the seat of his trousers.

36

Dark Fibres of Dignity

Flagg stared into Charlotte's dull brown eyes with his own saliva smeared on his chin and lips, a trail of thin spidery splinters glistened a path from them to her breasts. Her chest rose and fell under her heavy breathing, her red ruby pendant swimming in a light seasoning of sweat. She felt paralysed like a fly in a spiders web after the first injection of serum from its fangs just before the feast of its numb flesh. Flagg stood abruptly his blade hanging limply by his side. With a swift bending motion he lifted the back of the chair a fraction and cut the bindings from her wrists. She could not feel them. They were worthless tools, even now. He lifted one of them above her head near a rusty metal hoop secured into the wall. He tied her wrist to this. She felt a numbness returning to her fingers free from their tight bindings. The black band of the wrist watch was covered in dirt and blood and for a brief moment it glanced the side of the metal hoop. The three powerful cyan lights triggered about eighteen inches from Flagg's face and unprotected gaze. The sudden blaze of the three lights flashed over and over again on the back of his retinas like a dozen flashbulbs in the dark. He held his eyes standing and drawing his hands to his face, his knife still an extension of his right arm. He stepped back. "Bitch!" He spat out and went to kick her in the face and head. Misjudging his position in relation to her his foot kicked out into thin air. A gust of cold air pushed past Charlottes face as she turned her head sharply to the left. Flagg fell backwards trying to claw the air for purchase, the knife falling from his grip and into a gully between the hollow chair seat and a wooden horizontal strut that was running parallel to it. Its handle thick and heavy struck the concrete floor first, leaving the blade protruding three inches above the chair leg. Flagg continued his descent and finally found purchase against the upturned chair. The knife pierced the right side of his ribcage and ruptured his aorta almost immediately. He signed and his body went limp. Charlotte looked at him passively and gulping she placed her head against the cold ragged wall. The concrete now did not feel so bad. She lay there for about twenty minutes, the dead weight of Flagg against the chair and her bare thighs. Her thoughts turning to Sabian and Brunner she lifted herself and manipulated her bra back on properly with her twisted and immobile fingers. She then picked at the binding to her other wrist until it gave way, her wrist falling and the sapphire crystal of the watch face smashing against the ground. Sitting herself up was a painful experience. She pushed Flagg off her who turned as he fell revealing the ivory bone grip of the knife sticking out of him. She spent the next five minutes bouncing herself on the chair to reach the grip of the handle. The vines around her ankles were too tight and she could not free them with her crippled hands and weak grip. Eventually she reached the handle and had to use both her wrists together to grip the thing where she inched it out of Flagg. It made a deep sucking noise as it finally exited and fell to the floor with a clatter. Collecting the knife with her stronger and more determined fingers she hacked at the bindings around her swollen red and bloodied ankles until they fell from her like used wet tissues onto the floor. She pulled the ripped remains of her dress over her aching and damaged body to restore the last dark fibres of dignity. Finally she stood shaking and shivering in the dark with the body of a man at her feet and a bloody knife in her hand. 'Was he a man; or a phantom from hell?' She thought as she stepped over him. Her teeth chattered as she pulled open the door and entered the long dark corridor that snaked off to the right. Walking with a limp she started to move a little faster, her bare feet echoing, the bottoms of them slapping the hard wet surface of the foreign and dangerous territory.

37

BAD666

Sabian's trousers were ripped in several places now and the tattooist's needles had started to weave a design on Brunner's trouser line as well, just as the door burst open and the slight rag doll form of Charlotte entered. She immediately used her feet and free hand to push the barrels and their lethal cargo of spikes from under the two of them, just as Sabians vine snapped and he hurtled to the wet floor. Sabian breathed a sign of relief despite not being sure if the impact of the chair had broken his neck or spine. There was a heavy ringing in his ears he was not happy about. His chair had remained upright in the descent. Charlotte without speaking set about cutting Sabian's vines. Sabian jumped to his feet and running to Peter's chair held it in mid air. "Quick the vine!" Charlotte swung Flagg's blade slaying through the vine. Peter's chair fell slowed by Sabian's cushioning of its elevation. Sabian took the knife from Charlotte and set about removing Peter's bindings. She kissed Peter lightly on the cheek. "Thank God, you're both okay!" she said in a broken voice staring into Peter's tired eyes. Peter stood speechless and his legs shaking and flicking his head from side to side to get rid of the dirty water from his ears and hair. The three of them ran and hobbled through the corridor where they finally came to a door opening without a door and shafts of dusty light inside. The light was coming through closed wooden shutters which Sabian peered through momentarily and then hastily tore open. There was about a twenty foot drop on the other side onto a derelict piece of sandy dead land that was covered with dying vegetation. Two old cars sat at forty five degrees to each other about twenty five feet away from them. There was no sound of crickets here just stark silence. Sabian was already running through his head the possibility that one of them may start up. Without talking Sabian lifted himself on the frame of the opening and lowered himself with both arms so he hung over the side allowing himself to drop in a controlled manner. His knees bent on impact as he fell into a soft roll to absorb the fall. Nothing bruised or broken he stood silently with both arms outstretched indicating with his hands for the others to follow. Peter helped lower Charlotte and Joseph helped catch her. Then it was Peter's turn. He lowered himself over the side and whilst he clung to the shutter frame with both arms outstretched Charlotte said "Be careful Peter!" Peter dropped cranking his left ankle which twisted with a sickening crack. The area around his ankle quickly filled with fluid as he sat silently writhing on the ground holding it with both hands. He hobbled to his feet, a sick and terrified look on his face. There was a sudden sound of crickets in the hot balmy summer air. There was no air to breath. Sabian eyed up the two cars, an old Ford Consul that was riddled with rust and all four tyres flat. It had no seats. Next to it was a newer dark coloured Mercedes. The door was not locked and when he opened it a deplorable smell of death and decay hit the three of them like a wall.

"Get in, don't argue". He said ushering the two of them forward. "I think I'm going to be sick." Peter said just before he vomited several times into the arid sand. His stomach heaved a couple of dry retches that tore at his throat muscles. He then fell into the backseat of the car next to Charlotte. Sabian was busying himself with the ignition cowling which was quickly and efficiently followed by the sound of sparking and the starter motor kicking over. "Come on, come on.". The starter motor laboured again several dry broken revolutions and then kicked in, the great engine growling like the strike of a Spitfires propeller blade. "Yes, yes, yes!" Charlotte began clapping her hands frantically and soundlessly together. Peter's head bobbed half on the leather seat and half over the generous foot well. He did not speak. Charlotte noticed something in the footwall. She bent down and picked up a dusty silver chain. On the end was a silver .22 bullet. Scratched into the side was the name crudely emblazoned, 'Daemon Flagg.' She smiled to herself placing the gruesome find into her right breast cup. She mused to herself the origins of the thing. He obviously thought if he had a bullet with his name on; no one else would, she thought. 'He who lives by the sword dies by the…'. The car jerked forward ripping its axles clear of the grass and vegetation that had spent a millennia growing into the bearings and soaking up the oil. The car jerked, spurted and backfired and finally the Spitfire engine kicked in again. The car moved forward ripping up the dust and sand as Sabian swerved it to face away from the complex and get them as far and as safe away as possible. The last thing that could be seen as the car tore through the dust were the letters of the registration plate BAD666.

BAD666 tore through the network of roads of the woods back toward the Grand Baie. Peter lifted his heavy head. "Where are we going, I'm not well?

"Somewhere safe!" came Sabian's reply. Charlotte rested her hand onto Peter's forehead.

"We'll be alright Peter, we'll be alright!"

Soon the three were inside the relative safety of the Calista. Sabian closed the saloon type shutters and slated doors pulled down the metal shutter and turned the air conditioning on. Peter lay on a side seat breathing hard and elevating his leg and ankle against a low TV stand. Beads of sweat formed and ran from his cheeks. Charlotte lay on the opposite seat in a similar mess although not in as much pain. Sabian looked tired as he busied himself. Dark circles were under his eyes and the seat of his trousers were all torn out. He still had fight in him but he was feeling the strain with each passing minute. "We all need rest. We shall be safe here. I need to get out, things are moving a bit faster than I anticipated." Said Sabian. "I need to get in the Marimba factory and start working." Charlotte sat up slightly, "But Joe you need rest, just take a look at yourself in the mirror for gods sake." Peter was now obviously asleep and starting to snore. Charlotte had a look of resignation on her face as she lay back down. "I killed somebody today" she said in a half whisper. Sabian stared at her sharply.

"Who?" Peter stormed. She let the battered bullet shaped pendant drop from her hand swaying like a pendulum. "Flagg, I killed Flagg."

"He doesn't even qualify as a human" said Sabian. "Where did you get that?" he continued leaning forward. "Back of the car we hot wired." Sabian was already leaving the boat. "I've got to dump the car before it's spotted. Hopefully they'll assume we're all dead by now and Flagg won't be found for a few hours." With that Sabian vanished and several seconds later the turbines of the Spitfires engine started up again which soon faded into the distance.

Charlotte made two strong black coffees with the last of her strength whilst Peter continued to snore. She placed both cups down onto the small plastic moulded table and lay next to Peter. He stirred briefly in his sleep and turning placed an arm onto her. She didn't lift it away or move away.

Sabian dumped BAD666 in a small section of woods about a third of a mile from the complex they all had just escaped from. He then made his way on foot to find again the Marimba factory and Longinner if that was at all possible. He wanted Longinner, wanted him dead! The slower the better! He had acquired himself the spare Beretta from the Calista and three spare clips, each with eight rounds. He had a throwing knife strapped to his left arm under his shirt and the will of the devil running through him. A primal evil instinct to kill!

Six minutes of running and he was back at the edge of the woods overlooking the great auditorium. The sound of crickets hammered a wall of noise in the background. 'Why have I come back here? What the hell am I doing?" he whispered under his breath as he checked the Beretta one more time, its clip firmly in place, but he knew this already. It was the third time he had checked it!

38

Crystal Skulls V Marimba Spheres

Maurice Longinner was dressed in his white ninja garb in a sterile room. Two ninja also dressed in white guarded a door behind him. He stared at six rows of crystal skulls that looked like bizarre novelties in a fun fair rather than technology with a potential for death. The rear of the crystal craniums reflected light like well crafted clear diamonds through their eye sockets each sending enchanted scatterings of rainbow prism lights onto the walls of the small room. Another ninja entered a seamless door from the left as if a hole of blackness had just opened up the same size and dimensions as a standard door opening. Then the room was perfectly white again and flawless without structural design.

"When will these be ready?" Longinner demanded.

"The final finishing process is not yet quite perfected sir."

"What do you mean? What the hell have you been playing at?"

"Sir we are still awaiting a communication from the Devlin cell in Montenegro. The skulls are bigger than the spheres and the density of the gel has to be changed."

"Well do it, do it man!"

"But sir, it's not that simple when we change the density to accommodate the greater viscosity something changes which we don't yet quite understand."

"What changes, what changes?"

"They don't -, work sir."

"Don't work!" Longinner's eyes narrowed into tight slits through the letterbox opening of his face covering. "What do you mean man, don't work?"

"Everyone's doing their best sir, all the cells. The rate of information exchange is nothing short of incredible."

"It is not good enough. They are supposed to be ready by the end of the week; otherwise we just have the spheres to run with. Six devastating explosions to rock this pathetic little planet."

"Sir, the Marimba Spheres will work just fine. I can assure you of that. The global cells are already to receive their final downloads so that they can upgrade their stock piles and software."

"I will have none of it! I tell you, none of it. It's the Crystal Skulls or nothing. Fail me and I will kill you Gruger. I will let Flagg have some leisure time with you. Do you understand?"

"Y-yes sir, the Crystal Skulls it is."

"Remember Gruger, fail me, and I will kill you. That is not a threat."

Gruger bowed with a short dip of his head and shuffled off into the automatically opening abyss that served as door.

Gruger entered another similarly bland and bright environment where six white ninja worked along a production line. In here they wore tight fitting goggles and face masks. Gruger had put his on as he entered removing them from a clip on his lanyard belt. A network of clear tubing pumped various fluids and compounds in a rage of rainbow colours. Gallons of the fluid from several overhead tanks marked with skull and crossbones and various hazchem symbols marked the start of the tubing network.

The tubing eventually fed into a single reservoir in its own chamber. The chamber was constantly kept cool by a further network of surgical stainless steel pipes containing liquid nitrogen. The fluid here was now a blue gel with a thick viscosity which dripped at the rate of two cubic centimetres a minute into the small but expanding reservoir of death at the base of the chamber. The thick viscosity of the gel made it stay in one single yet expanding flat clump as it accumulated in the reservoir. A single temperature gauge dominated this small chamber. A large four by four organic crystal display readout was prominently displayed on the white wall opposite the tank. Six elaborate sensors, a combination of platinum and silver were attached to the tank with a remote control feed from each to the nearby display. The temperature held stable at sixty degrees centigrade. One of the ninja sat patiently watching the organic display. A CCTV camera also watched the display; a silent partner in waiting. Gruger went to a sterile rack behind a white zipped partition. Unzipping it he removed a clear Perspex clipboard. He tapped the top left hand corner of the thing and it illuminated a bright crystal display of figures and schematics. A large temperature read out dominated the top right hand corner of the board. It too declared sixty degrees centigrade in two inch unblinking green figures. He walked down the line of ninja inspecting each part of the process and the quality of each ninjas work. Every now and again he would double tap the board to alter and refine the data fields. None of the ninja looked at him. Their work involved the utmost caution and when he noticed the faraway look in the eyes of one of them the anger in his body rose like the heat from a funeral pyre. He marched to the figure and pinched the back of one of his hands through the silk white glove. "Come!" he screamed. The others did not look back. The ninja bowed momentarily toward Gruger and then back toward the production line. He then obediently marched away from it through the opening dark abyss in the sea of whiteness. Gruger followed. They passed through a sterile corridor and entered another room. A thick glass partition quickly fell into place separating the two of them. There was no escape from the white room, no furniture, no window or other adornment. The ninja quickly removed his goggles and face mask in urgent disbelief. He shouted something but his words were silent. Gruger reached into his silk garb and removed a Shrukian ninja star that had been converted into a pendent on a chain around his neck. He leant forward and inserted it into a panel at the side of the room. Turning it he pressed the large blue illuminated button. The ninja was now hammering on the reinforced glass. It did not shake. It did not make a sound. A sprinkler valve opened up in the ceiling. The hapless ninja looked up toward the ceiling and toward Gruger. He shouted and the mouthed words "No my god what are you doing?" Gruger remained expressionless. A single droplet of gooey sinewy blue gel dropped from the valve landing with a splat no bigger than the size of an English one pence piece into the middle of the white floor. The man was now down on his knees and praying for mercy toward Gruber through the glass. The blue gel began to spread to a thin offering the size of a ten pence piece. It was now almost opaque, with nothing more than a blue tint. Like a large disposable contact lens. Gruger impatiently tapped his organic display clipboard and the temperature remote sensor activated in the sprinkler. The small rooms temperature was rising by the second with the ninja's body temperature.

The ninja threw himself around in the room like a fly caught in a microwave oven with a hot dish slowly turning and twisting on the rotating glass plate below. Still the temperature rose. He had ripped his head covering off and beads of perspiration ran in thick rivers down his face. Gruger turned the crystal display clipboard toward the ninja. The temperature readout was now at eighty seven degrees centigrade. The ninja fell to his knees again with a deep sense of resignation on his face. He reached into the inside of his upper clothing and took out a brown leather tri-fold wallet. Opening it he stared at a colour photograph of his wife and child. The blue gel was starting to bubble lightly on its surface as he cast an unwelcome and fearful sideways glance at it. They then followed a brief soundless flash that vibrated the glass ever so slightly and then it was over. Gruger had looked away momentarily as he had forgotten to change into more appropriate eyewear. The flash lingered in his line of vision long after it had terminated its super nova. Looking back at the room there was blood smeared on the thick glass and white internal walls that in places looked slightly viscous. But nothing else remained. Gruger had a look of displeasure on his face as he checked and rechecked the readings on his clipboard. He tapped the clipboard several times and a sprinkler system came alive with water and a special cleaning agent to flush away the detritus in the white sealed room.

Gruger returned to the production line. The ninja workers did not look back to him as he entered. He spoke in a loud bellowing voice, "This batch is all wrong, it ignited before body temperature was reached. It is too unstable for its job. Put simply, it is not fit for purpose". Still the ninja did not respond. They worked on diligently not questioning the disappearance of one of their number. This behaviour had become acceptable within their group. They did not know each other by name, only by a bar code number with a letter prefix which was attached to their chest on the left side.

39

The Waterfall

Charlotte awoke in the long afternoon sun. Deep shafts of sunlight projected into the Calistas cabin through the slatted windows above. She was in a pool of her own sweat with one arm around Peter. He lay still, snoring. He was exhausted and dead to the world. His injured leg was balanced at forty five degrees on the edge of the television stand. His leg was turning black from bruising from his ankle to his knee. Charlotte stood and staggered toward the semi-circle shower unit in the corner of the cabin. Stripping she stood in the shower and felt the wonderful jets of water against her tired muscles. Peter stirred in his sleep. Part of his mind could hear the gushing of the water in the shower and in his mind it became a huge expanse of waterfall as his escape with Mercedes and Sabian still went on. BAD666 had stopped, its engine finally failing with a deep throated cough and splutter. They were all out the car and running in an instant in the middle of a deep dense forest. Pursued by an army of black silk ninja with each a pair of bright red lasers for eyes. They ran and ran and ran. Death stars and needles hissed and whistled past them as they ran to the great waterfall which tumbled before them in great sheets into a dark abyss. Its roar was now deafening as the three of them felt the coolness of its spray. Sabian and Mercedes did not hesitate. They jumped into the rush of the thing. Brunner hesitated and glanced down at the soreness of his feet and the cheap chaffing sandals that he could have sworn he had discarded much earlier. Much much earlier. Staring back at the forest he saw three sets of red firefly like eyes were almost on him. The connected forms were dark and foreboding, shimmering and not quite in focus. He closed his eyes and taking a step forward fell into the abyss. The water crashed around his ears and massaged his tired body as he plunged the great rollercoaster drop, his guts in his mouth. He had started to scream almost the instant he fell but the noise of his own fear was drowned out by the squall around him. He opened his eyes for a split moment and saw that he appeared to be catching Charlotte up. The sensation of falling then left him and everything was in slow motion with the sound switched off. He thought his ear drums must have perforated with the great pressure that was everywhere entombing him.

Charlotte had got out of the shower and wrapped a heavy white towel around herself. She poured herself a long glass of lemonade over a mountain of ice as she watched Peter sleep. She bent close to his face studying the lines and the flicker of his eye lids. She leant forward and touched his wrist, lifting his arm as it had fallen limply over the side of the seat. In his dream she also had taken hold of his arm as they fell. He turned to look at her fragile form and she leant toward him as if to kiss, but as she did so two deep dim pin points of red light reflected from the back of her retinas getting brighter until they engulfed Peter in their red fiery hell. "I love you Peter!" he heard her say.

40

Artifice Entry

Sabian had managed to get back into the huge complex. The white blandness of the buildings contrasted sharply with the boldness of the Great Auditorium on the edge of the woods by the bay. The sound of crickets was deafening. He approached the Auditorium using the other buildings as cover. Once at the Marimba plant he watched and waited for thirty seven minutes until a lone ninja carrying a small white wooden crate walked past. He placed the crate on the ground and started to input a seven digit alpha numeric code into the keypad of a door. As he was about to enter Sabian snapped to his feet and walked toward the figure. "Got a light dear chap?" The ninja turned with a surprised look in his eyes. Sabian smiled at him and cast him a glancing brachial strike with the heel of his right hand. The ninja's eyes fluttered like the images of a faulty fruit machine. He fell to the ground. Sabian dragged him through the open doorway and quickly disrobed him and tied him with bindings from his own utility pouch. Sabian slipped easily into the ninja silks and straightening himself up he walked with purpose down the narrowing corridor of fluorescent lighting. His pace was quickly hastened by the sound of a voice from behind. It was Gruger. "Dieppe, where is that crate I asked you to get?" Sabians mind slammed around wildly, 'The crate, why did I leave it?'

"Answer me man, don't just stand there!" Sabian turned toward him lowering his head and walked subserviently toward Gruger.

"How dare you not look at me when I address you". Sabian did not say a word. He used two fingers on his right hand to immediately poke the offensive eyes that peered through the opening in the head covering. Gruger fell back screaming and holding his face with his eyes closed fearing he was about to go blind. Whilst he propped himself against the wall trying to focus on six images of his attacker Sabian turned into him again with a brachial strike with the heel of the same hand. Gruger fell, unconscious. Sabian quickly discarded the identity tag he was displaying and replaced it with Gruger's. He then picked up the clipboard that was still limply held in Gruger's left hand. He stirred as the board was removed and Sabian brought the heel of his left foot sharply down against the bridge of his nose. It broke with a sickening crunch and Gruger slumped back further into a horizontal position, two red pipes of blood spatter soaking through to the surface of his head covering. Sabian stared at him briefly and pulled him into a prone recovery position so that he wouldn't choke and then he made off down the corridor toward the production line.

Maurice Longinner finished another twenty five metres of the swimming pool, the last of thirty lengths which he religiously swam every afternoon just after three. As he pulled himself from the water he smiled thinking how Sabian, Mercedes and Brunner were now no doubt dead. He was shortly to meet up with Flagg who he felt sure would spill the full story, neglecting to leave no little detail out. He never much cared for Flagg's debriefs. They were always coloured with wild fantasy and distasteful descriptions suitable only for a director of an elaborate snuff movie. But this time he felt he would relish his every line. He would let him take up the details of the disposal of the bodies. That would be good for him. Make him feel important. Longinner would no doubt give him a few quid for his troubles that he would of course share in the loosest terms with his cronies. Maurice was being paid handsomely for his part in all this and he would no doubt give Gruger some credit as well. The chemical formula of the Marimba gel must be shared with the other cells and sleepers very soon, or the synchronised bombings of six major cities worldwide would not go ahead. Of course it could always go ahead to some lesser degree. This could not happen. Her orders had been exact and cruel. He shuddered at the thought of failure and what that would mean to him personally. He would not be able to return to his former position. They now obviously knew in some quarters that he had betrayed them and his country. He would be a marked man for assassination by his own and of course torture by his current and last line management. He dried himself off and dressed putting on a crisp white silk shirt with silver points on the collars. He slowly did up the bootlace tie looking at his inquisitive reflection in the mirror. He then pulled on a pair of leather riding chaps which in turn were complimented by his white leather cowboy boots specially made for him by Johnson and Wagner out on the Cincinnati Strip. The spurs jangled as he placed the Stetson on his head and took the battered Motorola from his pocket and dialled Flagg's number.

"Blast it, where is he?" He dialled the number four times in all. There was no reply. Flagg's phone was switched off. Impatiently Longinner made his way on foot across the dusty arid complex of the Marimba factory and out buildings. He removed his hat and held it firmly in both hands close to his chest. He started to feel a dead weight in the pit of his stomach and a sick rising sensation of anger as he noticed that his old diplomatic car was no longer parked abandoned. Two lines of tyre tread indicated a quick and explosive escape from the derelict part of the site. The sand and foliage was rucked up in great mounds of gunky mess and oil. The marks and oil trailed off away from the complex and toward the woods. He felt the flash of blood in his temples and anger gripping him from all sides to the extent that he felt his big hands wanting to crush his Stetson. He tried hurriedly to call Flagg again but still no response. It was all too much. He threw the phone at the rotting Ford Consul its fragile plastic body exploding into a dozen pieces. He turned skyward his mouth opening as if to eat the sky, "Flaaaaagggg!"

41

Mannequin

Peter could hardly stand when he tried. His leg did not look like it belonged to him anymore. It was totally black with bruising from the knee to the injured ankle. It looked like the leg of a man dead for a week. Charlotte was not around. The Calista moved from side to side ever so slightly with his vigorous rocking motion to get himself to his feet. Once up he hobbled and hopped toward the sink area and made himself a Vermouth with ice. He felt ill. He could not remember the last time he had felt this bad physically, maybe he was thirteen or fourteen, that time he got flu real bad and spent three weeks in bed and lost two stone. He did not remember much of that time. He couldn't decide if it was the pain, the heat, sunstroke or fear that was making him feel ever so slightly delirious. Probably all of the above. Propping himself up against the kitchen units he waited breathing deeply, waiting for the alcohol to be fully absorbed. He hobbled and twisted himself back around and drank two more shots, gulping them down. His tongue became numb. It drenched every damaged sinew of his body, first hitting his stomach and then feeding out to the network around it. At least that's how it felt, like the injection the dentist gives you. That slow crawling feeling of the mixture as it crosses its point of invasion along the arm and hits the heart firing the network into numb unconscious oblivion. Once he had slurped the last dregs from the glass with his head as far back as it could possibly go he hoped to the shower unit. Standing under the head almost fully clothed he turned it on. The welcome cool avalanche embraced him as he leant back against the hard tiling. A sudden flash of his nightmare came back to him. The mist and spray of the waterfall was all around him again. He felt terror. Something from the nightmare was trying to come back. Part of his mind fought to seize it whilst the other half tried to push it away forever. He could see and hear the waterfall and now had a sensation of falling. It felt strangely pleasant. He opened his eyes and to his relief he could only see the thin frosted screening separating the cubicle from the cabin several inches in front of his face. He saw a dark silhouette of a woman busying herself several feet away near the sink. He felt better realising Charlotte was back and tidying up the mess he had just left behind.

"Charlotte!" he shouted out in a broken voice garbled by water. There was no response. The figure was definitely Charlottes. She seemed to be ignoring him doing some chore. Peter suddenly felt exhausted again and wanted desperately to sleep or even just to lie down. Placing his forehead against the frosted partition the water fed a thick stream down the slope of his nose. "Charlotte." He mumbled, the name trailing off. He lightly tapped against the Perspex to try and get her attention. He then closed his eyes again. When he opened them a second or two later a darkness had engulfed the shower cubicle. Raising his eye level he saw that Charlotte was very close to the Perspex, maybe an inch or two. She did not move. The silhouette was very dark and featureless. Peter felt afraid. The figure was staring at him only inches away. It was motionless. "Charlotte" he coughed again. Nothing. He slowly reached down to the partition handle and drew it open. He fell back at the sight before him falling to the hard porcelain and lifting his arms up. A naked female mannequin dummy with a greasy texture stood in the opening. There was an overpowering smell of decaying fish. The face was featureless, except the two glassy eyes had two dim red lights at the back of them that were starting to glow brighter. "My god, my god, what's happening, have I lost my mind?" The sound of water gushed all around him as he covered his eyes with both hands. Soon he could feel the heat and the bright red light pushing through the gaps in his fingers. Charlotte's voice, distant and low echoed throughout the cabin.

"I love you Peter!" it said.

His eyes snapped open. Charlotte was looking down at him.

"Did you say something?" he asked.

"No, I've just been watching you sleep."

He laid there, his head confused, trying not to look at her, fearful that this may just be another extension of his fevered mind. Soon he felt better. He did not mention his nightmare to her or anyone else.

42

Labyrinth Marker

Sabian had used Grugers swipe card at least half a dozen times as he made his way around the white sterile labyrinth. Each new door was a marker to his existence and slid open without noise and slipped back into its recess leaving no obvious seals. The corridors seemed endless and were featureless and without signage. As he hurriedly entered another corridor three ninja walked toward him. His heart leaped into his mouth, but they paid him little or no attention, one of them simply gave him a respectful bow as they drew parallel. Sabian swiped the tired worn card one more time. A hologram could still be seen on it when it was tilted to a certain angle with the name Donald Gruger and the word supervisor in red next to it. The door opened to reveal a large workshop area with a high thirty foot gantry above it. About twenty ninja worked along what appeared to him to be some sort of production line. Sabian slipped the goggles and face mask on that were hanging from a lanyard on his belt to fit in with the others and walked toward a set of four aluminium steps that dropped down to the shop floor area. A ninja from the production line glanced in his direction. Sabian beamed a hard fixed stare back through his slightly misted goggles and the ninja snapped his focus away in an instant. The clipboard Sabian was carrying suddenly burst into life in a flurry of colour, symbols and data fields. A large temperature read out flashed slowly on the organic crystal display as if to catch the viewers attention at all times whilst surveying the screen. Sabian thought that the clip board had activated remotely when he entered this area. Another damn marker to his presence. He walked the full twenty metres of the production line to a cluster of exits. He wanted to break into a run. His heart was beating so hard that it was causing the identification badge now on its clip to flutter like the wing of a butterfly caught in the breeze. He worked hard at his deliberately slow step and business like demeanour. It wouldn't be long before Gruger was found, bound and gagged in the corridor where he had left him only fifteen or twenty minutes earlier. Just by sheer chance he clearly saw a recess marked with Gruger's pass number on it. He swiped the card and entered.

Charlotte busied herself making Peter a strong black coffee. Peter drank it and felt altogether more human. His leg was swelling and was black and blue.

"Here take these". Charlotte held out two white tablets in the palm of her hand.

"What are they?"

"Just strong painkillers, that's all!" Peter took them reluctantly with his last mouthful of tepid coffee. He did not like taking tablets. He figured pain existed for a reason and taking tablets only camouflaged the pain so that we could do further damage to our bodies.

"You're a very sensitive man Mr Peter Brunner, aren't you?" She said with her head to one side staring at him. Peter cast a quizzical glance but did not say anything. She leant forward and gently moved some hair from his eyes and forehead with her right hand.

"Feeling better?"

"Yes, yes fine." She kissed him lightly on the forehead. He held her wrists and turned them over slowly inspecting the gorged red furrows and bruising. He kissed her lips with his. The prize has been won he thought to himself with a pleasing sense of victory. They drank some more and spoke very little over the next thirty minutes. Then standing she undid a clasp at the back of her dress that allowed it to fall to her ankles. She stood there wearing only her red ruby pendant on its gold chain. It was the most exquisite piece of jewellery Peter had ever seen; to be adorned and displayed in such a manner as it was. The painkillers had started to work and the Calista rocked ever so gently as small waves from the hulls motion lapped the side of the quay wall.

Charlote afterwards lay clinging to his chest and fumbling with the small silver pendant he was wearing.

"Who got you the St Christopher- another woman?"

"It's not a St Christopher – it's a St Michael – it's a present from people I used to work with"

"Oh that's a relief – I can't have you wearing trinkets from past lovers". With that she undid the clasp of his chain and slid the bullet pendant along its length.

"What's that for?"

"For luck! From me to you!"

43

'Novus Ordo Seclorum'

Maurice Longinner was beside him self with anger when he found the empty chairs in Flagg's make shift torture chamber.

"Flaaaagg!" He screamed at the top of his voice. His voice echoed throughout the tight network of corridors and came back like a boomerang at least three times. The damp and dingy place was a stark contrast to the Marimba plant which was less than a hundred metres away. This was Flagg's place, his domain. Flagg was like a sewer rat he thought. What had he done with Sabian and friends? What wild elaborate game had he concocted to see them off? The lady, the boss would not be happy if the job of their disposal had not yet been completed. Too many things had gone wrong already. When was she going to maker herself known to him? These were all questions that had been eating away at him for some hours. He knew when the time was right she would appear in the mist like an ancient ninja of distinction, a ninja of the highest order. He did not know what she looked like or even what nationality she was. He knew that when the time was right she would make herself known to him and thank him for his hard work and loyalty. More importantly he would be paid a kings ransom. He had been given strict instruction on how she would identify herself. He would be presented with a double bared gold ring with a rectangular sapphire. The inside of the ring would contain a Latin inscription "Novus Ordo Seclorum!" – meaning "a new order of the ages." These Latin words would also be said by the great lady herself. He felt the whole thing was terribly absurd in its cloak and dagger veiling. He looked forward to the day despite this, of the great union. The 'Greater Seal of Approval', from the Council of Ninja would become his. Alas, this was all still a dream. Real work still remained. "Where is Flagg?" he whispered menacingly under his breath, his teeth grinding together.

Sabian glanced nervously around the room, looking for clues, anything that would assist. It was dark and he had to turn the lights on from his watch. A single lap top computer sat in the middle of a white desk next to a photograph of Gruger in ceremonial ninja dress. A ceremonial staff on a small stand was displayed proudly in a horizontal position at the front of the desk. There were no cupboards or draws in the room. He sat himself into Gruger's chair and removed from around his neck a small box about the size of a matchbox. Illuminating the Ingersolls lights a second time he studied the organic crystal clipboard from all angles looking for ports or other sockets. There was none. He sighed and then activated the matchboxes Bluetooth search option. It scanned for several seconds and detected the clipboard as an accessible device. The box them projected by a single laser a red full sized QWERTY keyboard onto the flat white surface of the desk. Sabian immediately was able to navigate around the clipboards data fields and icons by use of his keyboard. When he double tapped on individual icons he quickly realised that everything was covered with encryption security devices. He turned the lap top computer on. It to required an alpha numeric security pass. It wasn't going to be easy. Sabian stared around the empty shell of a room with a desperate look in his eyes. He was going to have to look for another way to hack into the system. He had been promised that the laser keyboard would be enough to bypass most if not all of the added security. He sat hopelessly back into Gruger's chair. An alarm like a police car siren suddenly activated from outside the confines of the tight office. He shot to his feet. One of three things had happened, if not all. Was it Flagg's rotting corpse that had been discovered in his torture chamber? Was it Gruger still choking for air in a sterile corridor, bound and gagged in nothing but his yellow string vest and 'y' fronts or was it the absence of his good self, Brunner and Mercedes without three foot bamboo stakes inserted into their backsides. No time to ponder. Within a flash Sabian was back out onto the shop floor. This time the ninja were not so focussed on their work. Only two of them remained at their posts watching the large digital temperature scale at the end of the production line. The other ninja gave furtive sideways glances toward Sabian whilst the two at the temperature gauge did not turn or even blink. He walked with a deliberate confident pace toward a door marked 'sortie'. The glances from the production line followed Sabian like a Mexican wave as he glided past them the siren still screaming from the speakers in the gantry above. The glances sought some sort of guidance but not too much. Gruger had always believed he had taught his people well; and for every eventuality that they may encounter. Slackness or a failure to respond in an appropriate manner would not be tolerated and the ninja would of course failing in this respect find themselves in that room, -the testing room that no- one ever returned from. There was something about Gruger's gait and length of stride that pricked at some of them. But not for too long. He passed through the exit door without so much as a challenge or good afternoon. The relative safety of the corridor was filled with hoots and drones of the siren which were now deafening. A green strobe flickered with the sick embodiment of a cheap fairground ghost train, just before your car is sucked through the swing doors and into the heart of blackness.

Longinner stood with stark bemusement on his sallow face. His bursting fist still crushed against the mushroom shaped alarm toggle. His other hand fingered the thick black braiding of his hat which he was clinging onto in Flagg's makeshift sewer. The room was empty except for two discarded chairs and the bamboo spikes that still had not kissed the blood of their intended prey. His gums drew back over his teeth and he spoke to himself in the flickering green light, "Where is the spy, the tart and that filthy English policeman?" And, "Where is Flagg?"

Sabian hurtled down the corridor, his heart beating like a jungle drum. Finally he threw himself out into the dusty sunlight and dense Mauritian heat that hit him like a gust of ignited aviation fuel. As he ran he half stumbled in the sand and glancing behind he saw four ninja in pursuit of him. Gruger's been found, it's got to be, he thought.

44

Gruger

Gruger sat still bound and gagged in the middle of the testing room. He'd been removed against his will from the corridor where Sabian had left him. Three ninja stared at him with cold unforgiving eyes through the reinforced glass. Small lines appeared at the corners of one set of eyes, the only indication that he or she was smiling at Gruger. The same ninja reached out to the start button on the control panel of the nearby wall. Gruger tried to speak in desperation through the tight gag in his mouth, his eyes flicking from each letterbox opening to the other in some sort of expression of hostile authority, as if he could exert it over at least one of them, even now. A single droplet of gel, a single swirling orb edged out of the teat of the sprinkler valve and dropped into the centre of his furrowed brow with a delightful splashing noise that only he could hear. It felt cold and impotent as it broke the banks and valleys of his screwed up forehead running like a cheap hair product down his cheeks and flanks of his nose. His eyes darted left and saw the temperature gauge rising. He started to scream flaying his head from side to side trying to dislodge the gag that was so tight it caressed his tonsils. He bounced along on his backside toward the sheet of glass. It was not pain; it was terror in his face. His stomach heaved and he vomited through the sides of the mouthpiece. It sprayed a fine mist over the glass leaving a shape of two perfectly symmetrical butterfly wings. Another droplet of gel hit the floor behind him. The temperature gauge had already reached its ignition threshold and he closed his eyes tensing himself for the impending flash into oblivion. His bowels evacuated themselves in the same instant. But nothing. No flash. No pain. Was he dead, had he passed over already? He opened one eye. The three ninja were laughing and pointing at him. The great Gruger sitting in his own shit. One of them bent to the ground and lifted from the floor a small tub of simple blue hair gel that was now two thirds empty. The ninja turned it upside down and unscrewed the lid. The last gob of it hit the floor with a splat. Gruger passed out.

Sabian made his way through the woods like a cougar on heat, shafts of dusty light hammering through the trees. He glanced over his shoulder. The ninja were no where to be seen. A death star whistled past his left ear and embedded itself in the trunk of a nearby oak. Then another, and another. He threw himself to the ground dragging himself like a grass snake through the undergrowth. Ants and small spiders splayed like small corridors of ink over his knuckles and upper arms. Small outcrops of rock and ferna ripped at his body through the thin cotton garb. He rested his head against the thick trunk of the oak that had a couple of embedded flying stars in them. With the recoil of a Cobra he pulled them free from the splintered wood. In wild desperation he threw one of them back in the direction he had come from. A guttural groan came from about twenty feet away followed by a heavy dead weight falling with a dull thud to a densely covered undergrowth carpet.

45

Inner Sanctum

Longinner's shaking hand reached out and turned the grimy rusting handle leading to Flagg's inner sanctum. His blue tiger eye ring scratched the wood and he growled holding his hand close to his face looking for minor imperfections across the blue marble glacier like surface. Sighing, he turned the handle and entered the room. Flagg's eyes stood frozen in their sockets staring at a point just above Longinner's head. Several blue bottles buzzed around in the room. An oil slick of blood that had already formed a skin covered the floor. There was a strong smell of faeces and cabbage. He struck out with his foot as if he was kicking a football and flicked the side of Flagg's decomposing face. The head twisted violently with a cracking noise and a bloodless cut opened along his cheek from the kiss of his spur.

"Bastard amateur!" He muttered.

Peter was in the shower after Charlotte had helped him there. It was different inside to the shower in his dream and the inside view of Calistas main cabin was different too from his vantage point. Charlotte turned a radio onto a local station. A slow sax smouldered over hypnotic flutes and wind chimes. Peter had finished off the last of the painkillers with a large glass of coconut milk and ice. He felt sleepy safe and relaxed. The pain in his limb was a comfortable numbness. When he was finished he wrapped a luxuries white towel around his waist and Charlotte helped him back to the settee come single bed unit.

"Here!" She held out a long iced glass of lemon juice with a slice or orange and lemon over the rim. She dunked two bendy straws into it and playfully she ran her tongue over the edge of one of the straws. His gaze firmly fixed on hers. He sucked and she sucked. Once the glass was empty the remnants of ice popped and clicked as Charlotte placed it on the floor. She kissed Peter in a long lingering embrace of lemony wetness. That was the best fruit drink he had ever tasted he thought to himself as Charlotte started to unwrap the damp towel from around him.

When they had finished Peter laid back relaxed and content. Charlotte lay beside him in the blistering heat, her wet heaving body like a work of art; like a perfect moment in the whole of history. In the whole of Peter Brunner's history! It was a moment that defines a life; a marker; a magic marker in the milestone of a single human existence; Peter Brunner's existence. A small circular ceiling fan circled above as they lay holding hands in the fading sun of the day.

"I hope you are a single man Peter Brunner?"

"Very single, what about you?"

"As single as can be, what a wonderful situation."

"For a moment I thought you and Sabian might have had something."

"Perhaps there was a possibility of that once, but that was some time ago now. I think Mister Joseph Sabian is too wrapped up in his work. He sees all women as play things. I hope you don't see me that way Peter?" She placed her arm across his chest and pulled herself onto him, her soft wet curves gliding over his torso.

"No of course I don't see you that way. What would make you say something like that?"

46

Bianco Cellini

Sabian was still and panting in the undergrowth staring into the high trees and darkening sky that was whispering bye to the last shade of blueness. He was listening hard in all directions. The sound of the forest was alive, but he knew that the ninja moved like black widow spiders. Spiders were excellent creatures of survival and much older than humans; their species hardly changed; their instincts so well tuned and developed toward their own sense or mortality. Were the ninja the same, thought Sabian? He suspected that they were. There are over four tons of spiders to every human being on the planet and as Sabian nervously flashed his eyes from left to right he thought most of them are probably in these few square miles of island paradise. He suddenly felt paralysed with fear as he felt an animated dull weight scurry the length of his right arm stopping on the back of his hand. His heart missed a beat. Beads of perspiration had formed under his head covering. It stuck annoyingly to his forehead and cheeks. Moving his eyes down he saw the eight legged monster watching him, a rhythmic pulse shifting through its legs, two large fangs hanging below two neat rows of four eyes. It can smell fear he thought, no it can really, changes in hormone release, sweat output, it's a pheromone thing. He could take the tension no more. He did not want the beast under his clothing. An unthinkable state of affairs. Sharply he flicked his wrist and it tumbled through the air glancing an olive tree branch flicking its swirling legs into a new orbit some four feet away. It fell on its back and in a moment of super gymnastics was back on its feet looking back at Sabian its eight eyes fixed on him like heat seeking missile silos. Then it started to run back toward him, the heat signature a large target in its world of death and adventure. He could take it no more, ninjas or no ninjas; he was out of here so much. Ripping his face covering off he took to his feet and made to run into a clearing. He barely perceived the movement above him in the high foliage. Suddenly a ninja swung down from a branch hanging by his feet. The pursuing spider had given up, scrambling into a small webbed hole as the black silk covered apparition dropped into Sabians path. Sabian stopped three feet from the thing. He was thinking through his next move when an American voice, long and drawl came from behind the black face covering.

"Joseph Sabian, -Mister Joseph Sabian, Roger Folkestone, American Secret Service at your service!" With one hand the ninja removed his face covering and the other extended out into mid air toward Sabian. They surveyed the upside down image of each other that up to now each had only seen in highly classified documents. Sabian reluctantly held out his right hand and shook Folkestone's which was a bizarre and uncoordinated experience. Sabian touched Folkestone's cheek and turned his face still partially unconvinced. Folkestone dropped, somersaulting and falling perfectly upright on both feet. He was a man in his mid forties, six feet one, and had a small two inch scar above his left eyebrow. The two men now shook hands vigorously. Sabian felt a greater confidence now in his purpose and mission.

"I thought you were dead, what about Camilla?" asked Sabian.

There was a sudden flurry of movement from above. As Sabian cast his gaze upwards a black silhouette flashed by. Another ninja stood about four feet back from Folkestone and removed its head covering. Sabian smiled. Camilla Dufus smiled back. She stepped forward to shake the hand of Joseph Sabian. Sabian suddenly had an urgent anxiety on his face. "My god, what about the poor chap I hit with the metal star thingy?" Roger glanced at Camilla and Camilla spoke.

"He is a she, and she's fine. A couple of scratches that's all. We thought you were Gruger trying to escape from us. You're not hurt at all are you?"

"Only my pride!" replied Sabian. "Wasn't really sure who you were until that head covering was removed."Continued Roger.

"Where is your third member?" Sabian was already scanning the immediate vicinity of the woods. A figure emerged from behind a thick oak some twelve to fifteen feet away and Sabian was immediately spellbound.

Bianco Cellini a twenty three year old was five foot seven, blond hair flowing over her shoulders as she walked toward the huddle. Her mascara had run from a single tear. The top of her garment at the shoulder was ripped and blood bathed the area.

"My dear girl I'm so sorry!" said Sabian moving toward her.

"I can't stop the bleeding." Sabian already had hold of her arm and was inspecting the wound.

"I have something that will help." He said. Quickly he removed from his belt a small packet of grey powder. Ripping the seal open he started to pour it onto her shoulder.

"What is that?"

"Quick-Clot. It was developed for the military. It should take care of it in no time." Within a second or so the blood flow had been stemmed.

"Hello, I'm Bianco Cellini!" She said nervously as she held her right arm out toward Sabian limply. She half turned her face away as she did so trying to disguise the obvious; that she had been in some pain and crying. Sabian took the hand and lightly kissed the back of it.

"The pleasure is all mine."

"We must get away from here." Said Roger and "We'll try to make things a bit clearer than they are. Soon this place will be crawling with ninja. We're trained well but are only three. They are an army; and you Joseph, just in fancy dress." They all laughed. So did Bianco.

Gruger still bound and gagged, crying and shaking like a broken man stared at the glass partition and the empty room beyond. He looked back at the inert gel and he could still feel the cold stickiness on his forehead. He dropped his head and started to sob. Who were the ninja that would play such an evil trick on him? He did not know. Were they wearing identification number badges? He could not remember. Stark fear had erased all the small details and much of the larger ones. He could only remember their evil dark silhouettes. They were no id badges, he felt sure of it! In any case CCTV would have caught all their antics. Suddenly he got a flash of a laminate id in his head. A fleeting image with no detail. They would be punished later he thought. Saliva ran from the sides of his mouth in thin spidery sinews towards his bare knees. 'Why can't I remember?', 'What strange phenomena!' Of course Sabian if he was in his position would have known exactly what the phenomena were. It was commonly known as 'the weapons focus effect', which made witnesses totally unreliable when confronted with sudden acts of violence. Suddenly there a shadow behind the partition and Gruger looked up.

47

White Hot Infinity

Maurice Longinner was standing there looking down at him with the same look in his eyes that someone has when they have trod in something and want rid of it. Longinner flicked the intercom switch to its on position.

"What in god almightys name are you doing in there?"

Gruger tried to speak but instead just gagged on his mouth covering that had been forced back hard between both rows of his teeth so that they peered over the top of the cloth top and bottom, like two rows of a Great Whites.

"I see you can't speak, best way I suppose, I do however feel the arrangement should be a bit more permanent." With that he flicked a switch and walked away leaving the room and entering a long sterile white corridor. There was a single interruption in which he stopped walking where the closing crack of the door was lit by a thousand flashbulbs. The crack then swallowed the white hot infinity and he continued walking.

Joseph Sabian, Roger Folkestone, Camilla Dufus and Bianco Cellini sat huddled around a small camp fire in an underground dig out some fifty feet away from where

Sabian had originally discovered the three of them. The smoke from the fire filtered through a makeshift chimney where it ebbed out at a side port close to the pull of a breeze near a small stream where it drifted unseen along the path of the embankment and out into the bay further upstream. The smoke at this point was nothing more than soft shimmering gauze almost undetectable to the eye as darkness continued to fall.

Sabian explained about the discovery of the Datsun, the ring and evidence of foul play at the intersection and how they all had assumed that Roger and Camilla where now dead. Roger explained that they didn't really know the true identity of those killed at the roadside. They had heard of the incident and thought that the two murdered were from Longinner's own people. There was a lot of unrest within his organisation, and rule and respect for his authority was breaking down. Roger went on to explain that the Datsun and a number of other personal belongings had been stolen several nights before the killings, which they had not had an opportunity to report. In fact they had not been able to get any message back to America or the UK. Camilla put forward the theory that the killings had been staged to make others think that they had been killed.

"It certainly had the desired effect on you Joseph!" she finished off. She took another sip of black tea from a battered stainless steel cantina cup. Roger was of the view that Longinner actually believed he may have murdered himself and Camilla, because after this their lives had become much easier and levels of suspicion around the plant had lessoned to a certain degree. Sabian listened intently but his gaze kept flicking and wandering to the young Bianco who had been studying him with all the grace of a spectator in a zoo watching a grizzly bear eat.

"And what's your story Miss Cellini? How do you fit into all this?"

Bianco appeared shy and reticent playing momentarily with her mug between both her cupped hands.

"Well it's like this," she paused looking nervously at Sabian and then to the others.

As darkness fell Peter held Charlotte close to him. They had cheerfully bathed in each others sweat for some two hours and Peter believed that in all his years of marriage; perhaps in all his life he had never felt this content. He drifted off into a wonderful sleep. The last painkillers Charlotte had mixed for him had already hit the spot. He held onto her sweet musky smell as he glided down a rich kaleidoscope of light that embraced him all over. It was a pleasant journey. It would have been a perfect ending to an imperfect day. One in which he had nearly died several times over and then possibly just possibly found the love of his life. Just before the final curtain of consciousness was drawn across the vortex of colour he had a feeling of fleeting foreboding. Two red laser like eyes cut through the fog of his mind just before he was plunged into darkness; the place where no memories are made!

As the final rattle of the crickets signalled the ending of the day Maurice Longinner was in his office making plans and spending immersed time on his phone and on the net. 'The Lady' was not pleased. He knew there were assassins in his own ranks, let alone those associated with Sabian. He knew 'She' had the power to have him killed at any moment. He had just been a pawn in a big global game of chess. Would he ever meet this woman?

Did he ever want to? When finally he would be able to pick up his pay cheque for all this, he was out of here, - gone; that much was for sure! He had had papers made up already. He may have to resort to using them much sooner than he had intended; and without his money. That would simply not do! Not do at all! He brought his fist down like a hammer onto the table, staring wildly at the blank white wall. What was he to do, what? He thought long and hard and finally decided on a plan of action. He would brief everyone the following morning. He would say that he had killed Flagg and show them CCTV of Grugers death. He wanted to get the message across to them that he was not a man to mess around with. He was not a man to upset. 'The Lady' would be pleased with that.

48

Brunners' Doubt

Peter's eyes opened slowly. The Calista was in darkness. He felt the soft sway of the water underneath the hull. It was three twenty seven am. Charlotte was not in the cabin. He spent the next twelve minutes looking for her, lower and upper deck. Not easy for someone in his condition. She was gone!

He stood on the upper deck holding onto a cold steel safety rail looking across the bay. The lights from the houses and yachts cast a rainbow of fragmented fluorescent colours dancing in a ghostly fashion on the black canvass of the water. He hobbled to a nearby deck chair and flopped into it. The pain of just walking had made him break out into a drenching sweat. His face and upper torso flushed red whilst his ankle felt like it was going to explode with the pressure of downward fluid on it. He was really no good to anyone now! How devastating and annoying! In this place less than forty eight hours and now this. His mind was a muddle of images and emotion. At least he wasn't dead, he thought to himself. The sudden realisation that he was not free from this living horror film entered his mind. Still not free from the possibility of danger. He wished he was back in England, behind his comfortable desk looking across Victoria from his high window at the Yard, watching the traffic light phasings and sifting through another orange docket. The rich smell of coffee from his De Luiseno filter clung to his nostrils as if it was on the actual deck with him. Finally he would drift into the sea of oblivious commuters, robots to a cause and eventually reach home, the safety of his Greenwich apartment. Once there he would take a shower, grab a bite to eat and prepare for a weekend evening out with friends around the local bars and restaurants. Far from the danger, the cut throats and bigots of the world. How he wanted that more than anything else. Anything but be in this wretched place with Sabian; and where had Charlotte got to? She was the only penny in the pudding in all of this; this whole affair! He wanted her badly, but did not know how to say it or convey it. He felt, despite their evening that she only had an eye for Sabian; the all man of action. Was she on the rebound he wondered? What has happened to her, has she been kidnapped? Stolen by ninjas? Perhaps she was now dead. For a brief moment the thought horrified him; her limp white staring bloodied corpse in some damp dark room where it would stay for an eternity, bloating and stinking; a feast for the flies and crickets. Panic all at once rose in him and he felt a desperate need to run away; if only he could. He wanted to get away from the Calista as far as possible, and anything connected with Sabian and this mission. He needed somewhere he felt safe, and it wasn't here! He also wanted a soft double bed and blackout curtains that would hide him from this new and dangerous world. 'I must get away, must get away, it's not an option!' He stood by catapulting himself with the full force of his lower arms and wrists against the chairs armrests. The excruciating pain was back but now he felt purpose running through him and adrenalin helped him overcome. Not to stop or lessen it; to ignore it!

Half an hour later he had managed to hobble into the foyer of the Apex Court Hotel; using a steel pole from the Calista as a makeshift crutch. The man in the suit behind the reception desk looked on in horror as the fragile figure made its way to his position across the great expanse of marble flooring. Each step was sounded by a metallic heavy clinking of the unprotected and sharp circular edge of the pole against the expensive flooring. Brunner looked up at the unwelcome eyes; one raised in speculative disgust.

"Now that wasn't so bad was it?" Peter said, breathing rather heavily.

"And what can I do for you Monsieur?" The voice had a brittle condescending tone about it.

"I would like a room if that's possible, nothing fancy."

"We are fully booked at the moment. I am sorry!" The man's beady like eyes shot him a curt like glance from the tip of his toes up to the last hair on his tired head. Fleeting, but there nevertheless. Brunner did not respond. He glanced over his left shoulder at four empty high back brown leather studded club chairs.

"I'll take one of those seats until morning then!" As he turned the man noticed the rips in the seat of his trousers. His hand hovered over a phone just out of view as Brunner glanced back giving him a hard stare. Just as he was about to drop his half exposed backside into the leather high back. "Oh Monsieur, yes I think I do have a room after all!" Brunner stopped and stared at the man who was nervously and frantically picking up a large red leather bound ledger type signing in book. He opened it with a thud and as Brunner clunked and clinked his way back to the counter the man ran his finger up and down one of the thick vellum watermarked pages.

"Oh yes, here we are." Peter leaned against the high mahogany support of the circular counter. The man's face screwed up in a silent wincing motion as the steel pole clanged against the floor in accidental freefall. There was a pregnant silence.

"Well, do you have a room?"

"Yes, but it's the equivalent of five hundred pounds a night!" With that the man had an insidious look of right-eousness on his face, a rich smugness that he was wearing like a badge of honour. Peter started to pat his pockets at first speculatively and then nervously. My god, no wallet! The man's badge of honour expression grew more hopeful as an amused grin cracked his face. Brunner suddenly had an idea and started to unbuckle the thick brown leather belt of his trousers.

"Ah Monsieur, what are you doing? I will call the police if you do not stop!" Peter suddenly placed the belt onto the glossy mahogany counter whilst he held his trousers up with his free hand. The inside zip of the security belt was clearly visible, but he was unable to let go of his trousers. He gestured with a nod toward the zipper, and the man behind the counter lent forward lifting the belt as if it were someone's smelly sock he had just found in his own laundry basket. He dropped it back onto the counter in disgust. Peter again picked it up and clamped his teeth around the inner zip and gently drew it down pulling with his hand. As he did so four self seal polythene bags dropped to the floor. The man behind the counter stood frozen like a statue unable to make sense of the stranger. Peter stood back from the counter, gesturing to the bundled bags on the floor.

"I think you'll find it's all there!"

"All there, what sir? What are you talking about, all there indeed?"

"I can't bend to save my life here mister, so you're going to have to help me out a bit. You'll have to pick them up. Each bag has about two hundred in cash. Give me one of the bags back and you can keep the hundred in the last bag. That's your tip! Now, where the hell is this room, I'm close to collapsing and I need a shit?" With that the man hurried himself from behind the counter walking with an almost mincing action. He leant and picked up the bags and splayed them open on the counter. Four bundles of crisp notes rolled out. He counted them out into a single pile with the efficiency of an experienced banker or croupier; thumbing through them and occasionally wetting his forefinger and thumb. He creamed off the top five bills like a magician palming a card and slid it into his back pocket with a wiggle. He then reached behind him and took key number seventy six of its brass hook and held it out at arms length like he was holding a rat by its tale. Brunner had finished rethreading and fastening his belt and snatched the key. Brunner's gaze cut the man off as he headed towards the lift.

Closing the hotel door behind him he hobbled to the bed in the middle of the room. It had fine oak supports and posts that dominated the medium sized room. There was a smell of fresh jasmine with a hint of vanilla. The décor was simple yet expensive. A small highly polished Queen Anne desk graced the side of the room closest to the window and veranda. It had a single green glass banker's lamp with thick bevelled brass stand on it.

A similar brass lamp with a more subtle white glass shade sat on the bedside table. A Matisse print graced the wall at the foot of the bed. Brunner flopped onto the bed and felt the welcome embrace of the mattress take on his contour; his heavy torso and limbs supported in space age comfort. He pressed his right hand into the mattress and for a split moment in time its impression lingered when he moved his hand, like a jelly mould waiting to be filled. He laid back and closed his eyes. He felt safe, but like a wounded animal that had beat a painful and hasty retreat back to its lair. Yes that was it, he felt wounded. His mind swirled, faces, visions and flashes running through it. Excited delirium was setting in. Wounded like an animal, a fox so cautious and helpless from the woodmans snare. Alone; the door at last closed on the big bad world.

49

Aphrodite Plazza

Bianco Cellini was still staring at Sabian over the battered rim of her cup, steam gently rising past her beautiful face and flowing hair.

"Well come on then!" said Sabian, "Don't leave me in suspense!" She tried to crack a smile which didn't quite make it and then took another hurried sip of tea that barely wet her lips.

"I work at the local, - did work at the local bunny club!" Sabian's right eyebrow raised half an inch furrowing his forehead on one side. There was a silence and another hurried sip followed by a nervous glance toward Camilla and Roger and then she stared back at him.

"I've been doing the tables at the Aphrodite Plazza for about eighteen months. I just kind of got wrapped up in all of this. The club's owned by Maurice Longinner, although that's not the official name on the letter headings and tax returns. He took a shine to me and tried to make advances. I wasn't having any of it! He didn't want me to work the tables anymore; couldn't stand other men pawing over me. He got me started on a bit of book keeping and secretary work for him. He increased my pay but was still trying to come onto me. I knew his game, I was just waiting and watching, biding my time, make enough money and split the joint. One night we were in his office at the back of the club. One of the girls didn't show. He was angry and wanted me out on the tables for the evening. I did it reluctantly. He had threatened not to pay me for the month I had just worked. After the night on the tables I went to his office. He was staring wildly at me, the same look I see in the punters eyes night after night. He pinned me against the wall. He was going to rape me. Then that insane character Daemon Flagg turned up like a bad penny. I heard Flagg say something like, "Let's wet the bitch up!" He was holding a knife and I was terrified. I started to scream, I couldn't hold it anymore! Two ninja all in black burst into the room, didn't speak just pulled guns the two of them, couldn't see their faces or anything. Longinner and Flagg backed off. That was the last I ever saw of those bastards. I was placed into a speedboat and we were off across the bay." Roger chipped in- "and she's been working with us ever since." Sabian said "I take it—-"he pointed a scoping finger backwards and forwards between Roger and Camilla. "Yes, it was us. Didn't want to blow our covers still with Longinner or Flagg. Just our trusty old service revolvers and an air of menace, none of that kung fu type shit, we'd have got our arses kicked for sure!" Sabian looked at Bianco almost studying her, "and why were you working in that dive in the first place?"

"It pays well with tips and all. I was saving so I could move away from this hell hole island, move closer to my grandmother in Sweden."

"I did detect a bit of an accent, not much though" said Sabian.

"My grandmother is really ill with leukaemia. She's not expected to live the year. Her treatments are very expensive. I just want her to be as comfortable as possible."

"That's very admirable, but there are plenty of other things you could have turned your hand to I'm sure, without resorting to ...

"With a body like this, what do you think is going to pay more Mister Sabian, me waggling my booty in high heels or scanning tins at the local Wall Mart?" She stared at him with a wall of fire behind her soft blue eyes. He glanced down embarrassed and lost for his next sentence. She rose quickly and threw her half empty cup to the ground where it clattered, minuet spay flicking over Sabian's fingertips. She indignantly started to walk toward the step ladder.

"Where are you going?" Roger asked.

"For a piss,-okay!" No one answered as she pulled herself up the ladder and into the woods. Sabian looked up at the others.

"How much does she know about all this?"

"Enough to see her and us through" said Camilla.

"Bits and pieces, not the full shooting match" continued Roger.

"She's a bit of a fire cracker isn't she? I like her!" Sabian revealed.

50

Room Service

As Brunner awakened shafts of golden light splayed through the slits in the shutters cutting their design into the room. He looked at his watch. It was eight thirty am. He did not care that the others may be concerned about his whereabouts and welfare. He was passed all that. It was all a simple game of self preservation and that indeed was what it quite literally meant, self self self. He did not want the feeling of security and warmth that had engulfed him since entering the hotel room to leave him. He wanted to keep his own destiny within his own making and no one else's. But he knew that this feeling would not last and that at some point in the day he was going to have to break his cover of security and flee into the world; maybe try and get a flight out of all this madness. He would have to locate his passport. He was not even sure any airline would take him in his current condition. One thing was sure, he was ravenous again. He leant forward toward the bedside table where he could see a glossy hotel brochure and menu amongst the complimentary envelopes, note pad and pen. He was still in a lot of pain, which had now extended into the whole of his body like a mild flu virus. He opened the brochure and quickly ran his finger down to the section marked room service. He ordered himself a carafe of black coffee, toast and extra thick marmalade, a bowl of fresh figs and sweetened Greek yoghurt.

When the knock came at the door about twelve minutes later he flinched and sitting up he slew his legs horizontally over the side of the bed and using his stick hopped to the floor in a standing position.

"Who is it?"

"Room service, your breakfast is here, yoghurt and figs!"

Brunner stood back from the door in the corner of the room raising the steel stick above his head in a recoiled defensive position. He then tepidly leant forward and drew the bolt back from the door, and opened it an inch with the chain still on. It hammered into its open position against the strain of the chain and the force of the food tray. He slammed the door shut.

"Just leave it outside on the floor. I'll collect it in a minute; sorry I'm not decent at the moment." There were several seconds of silence followed by "Very well monsieur, as you wish!" This was followed by further movement as the tray was placed down onto the carpet outside the door.

"Would sir be requiring a newspaper?"

"No sir would not!" At that he slid down the wall to the ground. He started to sob.

He stared around the room through his bleary eyes. Collecting his thoughts and emotions he opened the door and dragged the tray along the floor and gorged himself on the feast where he sat. When he was finished he rested his head against the hard wall and aimlessly stared at the Matisse on the far wall, an expanse of gaudy yellows and greens with an expensive heavy looking gilt frame. He went back to the bed and fell on it. He had until one thirty before he would have to vacate the room so he intended to get his every penny's worth. He fell into, despite the circumstances a deep dreamless and contented sleep.

When he awakened it was just before noon. His ankle felt numb and he was able to put pressure on it with much less pain. It was nearly time to face the music, time to face the world he had been hiding from in his self.

Shortly after twelve fifty he was out again in the street, keeping to the building line and in the shadows. He was shivering despite the heat and he felt like a down and out hobo. He reluctantly made his way back to the Palm Hotel where he had left all his belongings on first arriving at the island. Was it really only two days earlier? He had hidden his passport there; despite orders to the contrary by Sabian and Charlotte. And what about Charlotte Mercedes; did he want her that much, did he need her? Her face and beautiful eyes hung in his mind with her soft lingering curves. She smiled at him. I think that's a yes Peter dear boy, he thought. Suddenly he felt guilt sweep through him. He didn't know if she was safe or not. He didn't know how Sabian had got on at the Marimba plant. Last night he didn't care, had passed caring. The previous nights instinct for self preservation was now eating at him; the selfishness of it all. But what could he really do under the circumstances the little voice in his head moaned, stay at the Calista and possibly be at the bottom of the bay by now, chained down with concrete wellies for footwear. Perhaps that was where Charlotte was already, the fish already swimming through the channel of her nose cavity to her throat and down through the valley of her cleavage. No it was the right decision; yes it was right despite all the other ramifications.

Charlotte had entered the Calista with a supply of more painkillers and other supplies the previous evening and found Peter gone. Her initial thought was that he had been kidnapped. She spent an agonising ten minute search of the yacht and the water around it to make sure he hadn't fallen overboard. Perhaps he had, he may have drifted. She then against all her instincts went to the Palm, but of course he was not there. Returning to the Calista she lay in the dark of the cabin, a strange tension invading her whole body, between fitful episodes of sleep and sudden wakefulness as if an invisible gong had gone off in the room. Of course it was totally quiet, still and dark. If only she had stayed with him in the safety of the yacht. Soon her tired body drifted into slumber.

She was wakened with a start; almost like the passing of hours had happened in a blink to see Peter hobbling through the door. He glanced at her face as she wiped the sleep from her sticky eyes. There was an air of conspiracy and suspicion in the cabin, each wondering what the other had been up to. Peter made his way with his home-made crutch to the opposite sofa bed and flopped his full body weight down. The Calista shimmered in its anchorage. He lifted the damaged leg onto the soft cushion of the mattress and then lay back staring at the ceiling with both hands clasped across his chest. He had a look of indignation. Charlotte detected it.

"Where did you go?" she said softly.

51

Commissioner Charles Blake

Dacres sat in the darkened office lighting his third cigar in twenty minutes. The air was filled with dense thick smog that clung to the curtains and his double breasted crisp suit. He sat back in the Wagner high back leather club chair looking at Charles Blake, Commissioner of Police across the green blaze of his desk. Blake's forehead was deeply furrowed and the side of his nostrils slightly flared at this third act of indignation and selfishness. Dacres leant forward and snapped open the mahogany well worn cigar box with its little strange faded copper inlaid symbol on its lid that Blake felt convinced was something to do with freemasonry. He didn't have much time for masons.

"Care for one, they're Havana specials?"

"No thank you. Can we just get down to it, what am I up against?"

"Mister Blake I've lost contact with my entire unit out in Mauritius. I've not heard from any of them in days. It's a rather worrying situation! We both know the possible dangers here."

"When can we expect activity to start?"

"By activity Mister Blake I'm assuming you mean the bombings to start?"

"Yes, that's what I meant."

"I'm hoping never, but everything suggests bombings, co-ordinated bombings will take place in six major cities worldwide."

"When?"

"You saw the docket and the presentation at the select committee gold group meeting, as I did Mister Blake. Nothing is for certain or an exact fix, we only know that the threat is imminent and very likely. What provisions have you made since our last meeting?"

"All police leave has been cancelled for the foreseeable future and I've had a number of gold command meetings with all the heads of the emergency services and armed forces. There's also a lot of local authority and private sector involvement, makeshift mortuaries and refrigerator lorries from haulage firms mainly. Of course they are not aware of what we are facing here. That would be totally unacceptable. They have merely been put on standby and given rendezvous point locations for the setting of the haulage equipment, as part of a pre planned arrangement for this sort of operation. In a nutshell to them it's just another drill. We scramble them and many other partners every several months or so to keep everyone on their toes. This will feel no different, and will certainly not be out of place."

"Very good Mister Blake!"

"Is this going to be anything like the V cell virus scare eighteen months ago which amounted to nothing; after it was discovered that it would take an individual to eat about two pounds of the compound for it to have any ill effects and actually infect? Even then it was no guarantee of infection!"

"Mister Blake we stopped the V virus forty five minutes before it was about to be placed into the three main reservoirs feeding everything within the M25 area. It would have only have taken one person to have been infected, become a host carrier and then we would have had a deadly epidemic on our hands. It was a success, but the ball was too close to the net for my liking. I do believe that my goal keeper and yours I might add are getting tired and have started to develop sores on their cold and blistered hands from catching these balls."

"Yes, you are right."

"We need to develop continuously new and innovative ways to break down the barriers. I have my best operative on this at the moment, Joseph Sabian. I do hope your Mister Peter Brunner is of equal standing within your circles as Sabian is in mine?"

"He's okay!"

"Just okay maybe not enough. I hope he's a good goal keeper Commissioner, and that his hands are not covered in calluses just yet; metaphorically speaking!"

"He's a good man. I've seen his file and met him several times. He has a strong line management and I have complete faith in him and them to deliver the goods."

"Is he a likely candidate to be turned and become native Mister Blake? It was an important and relevant question posed by one of the delegates at the Gold meeting some weeks ago. It can be a problem. We have not heard from Sabian or Mercedes, and you have not heard from your Peter Brunner. And equally as worrying the CIA have not heard from their operatives. Something very wrong has happened. There is a ghost in the mist yes?"

"Are you asking me a question or making a statement?"

"Perhaps both Mister Blake."

"Have you considered sending a back up team?" continued Blake.

"If you remember Commissioner that point had been agreed about three years ago. Perhaps you personally have not been briefed on this aspect as it was your predecessor who had a hand in the final policy development; but you should be familiar with it. There was already another team out in Mauritius who were meant to be shadowing the others, but again they to have fallen off the radar. We are totally blind and dancing in the dark. Some of our best, if not the best people are missing in action and that is not good, not good at all! I've noticed Mister Blake that you keep eyeing this cigar case; the symbol is of interest to you perhaps? I am not a Freemason Commissioner. Please don't worry that the press are going to make of me and you as anything more than withholding to the highest levels of integrity."

"I didn't think you or I lacked that for even a second!"

"Ah yes, but we both know that the hounds of our society and the media will make of things as they want and when they want and for their own ends. I don't know how they sleep at night. I sleep soundly at night myself, how about you Commissioner?" Blake did not answer as Dacres stood and walked to the window staring out across the buildings and streets, a thong of activity that raged day after day, but for how long?

"Things could all change Charles. We must be good, keen and professional goal keepers. Infact we must be better than even that! The punters should not even get through the turnstiles; the players out onto the pitch, do you understand where I'm coming from?"

"Yes, perfectly"

Dacres seemed far off in his thoughts as he took another draw on his cigar. He then walked stolidly to a steel filing cabinet and entered a six pin number into a keypad. A second later he removed a black file bound in a white ribbon and gloomily walked back to his seat, his cigar still in his mouth. He puffed and sucked at irregular bouts balloons of smoke floating like mushroom clouds above a steam locomotive. He threw the file down onto the blaze and pointed with a wieldy accusing nicotine stained finger.

"In there Mister Blake is an own goal. Something failed in the vetting procedure. Something between your organisation and mine, the whys and the wherefores are not important at the moment. The Home Secretary has called for an urgent review meeting in less than the hour, so we'd better start with some mutually credible answers and strategies to rebut any fallout." He pushed the file toward Commissioner Charles Blake as if he was prodding a dead cat he had just run over. Blake undid the white ribbon that shackled the pages together. He opened the first leaf, read several lines and scanned a photograph.

"Jesus!" he moaned.

"You see Mister Blake nothing is at all well in our little undercover operation; suspicion of a mole has been on the radar for some time. It gives me no pleasure revealing these details to you."

Blake looked passively up at Dacres, the lines and furrows on his forehead deepening by the second.

52

Montage

Sabian walked toward Bianco. She was sat under the large oak that he had initially encountered the spider on his arm. Her head was down and her arms linked around her legs cradling herself.

"I am sorry about earlier. I'm not always that diplomatic. I do apologise!" She did not respond. Sabian wondered if she was crying.

"I wouldn't stay there too long if I were you, I encountered a very large eight legged hairy thing the last time I was just where you are now. I think he lives nearby and you're in his neighbourhood; it's not what I'd call a very safe neighbourhood!"

Her head raised slowly, her black mascara smudged with a double track of it running the full length of her marble face tailing off at her chin that was slightly shaking.

"I am sorry I reacted like that?" she said.

"No need to be, I'm sorry to."

"I hate Longinner, and I just want to get off this island." She continued.

"I think that feeling is totally mutual." With that Sabian outstretched a hand out to her.

"Come let's join the others." She took his hand and stood, following him to the dig out. She stared at the ground and didn't speak.

Longinner took the staff out of the holder and whipped it through the air of the auditorium. His heart was racing and sweat was running down his back. Great arc lights cast his shadow along the floor as he parried with it as if it were some other supernatural being. Suddenly he threw the stick in the air. It landed with an echoing fierceness as he dropped to his knees and raised his hands over the back of his head, his mouth and face turning toward the great apex above in a silent scream.

When Peter was fast asleep Charlotte tip toed to the bathroom so as not to disturb him. She took a small gold coloured key from a pocket specially sewn into her dress and opened the small mirrored medicine cabinet above the sink. On opening it she removed the only item, an aluminium and black rubberised case about six inches by four. She placed it on the floor between her legs. She closed and locked the door and started to reapply her make up from a disorganised array of pencils and containers in a small white bucket that hung by a bent coat hanger from the u bend under the sink. The experience was annoying her as she had to keep ducking to see her features in the reflection of the mirror of the cabinet that was partially obscured by an etched cross in a circle. She finished off the process by applying a dark purple lipstick which she put on vigorously. She kissed a tissue paper several times to get rid of the excess before discarding it into the toilet bowl. Slipping the dress off, she opened a black clothes holder that was hanging by the sink and took out a single one piece black heavy duty canvass jump suit. She slipped her legs into the holes and pulled it up over her body before zipping up the front. She picked the rubberised case up and placed it awkwardly into the recess of the sink and moved the three tumblers to the number nine one eight. It clicked open.

Inside was a single syringe and a phial pushed into sculptured foam recesses. She took out the unmarked phial of clear liquid and puncturing it with the needle she drew out the full content into the syringe. Her face had a determined look as she stepped back into the cabin where Peter lay asleep. She roughly took hold of his right arm and injected the full contents.

53

Hard Rain

When the rain falls in Mauritius, it falls hard, fast and without warning. Sometimes the only precursor is the blotting of the landscape as if there was an impending asteroid collision. This darkness had started to fall as a lone female in a black jumpsuit emerged from the Calista and lightly sprinted across the quiet road to a side alley where an old battered Facel Vega KH500 sat. She opened the drivers door using the key that had been held tightly in her fist; so tightly that it had now left a white and red outlined impression on her right palm, temporarily smoothing out the canyons of her life and heart lines. The car door sharply struck the neighbouring wall, chipping the already pock marked surface of its paintwork. She glanced at the central grouping of dials in the middle of the console as she fired up the front mounted De Soto Fire Dome V8 engine. It roared the pleasure of a lioness being teased with a five pound steak at the end of a pole. Its rev counter kissed the red line then quickly floated like the second hand of an expensive pocket watch to about a thousand revolutions per minute. The lioness now purred with a low growl in her throat slowly cantering in a circle and pretending not to look at the flesh at the end of the javelin. Mercedes floored the accelerator and the lioness roared with thunder as it attacked the bloody lump of meat. With the handbrake released the small blue car shot out into the main artery of road which was now gripped in darkness as the heavens opened. In an instant great sheets of water pushed down the windscreen. The tired wipers could hardly keep up with the intensity of the onslaught. Mercedes eyes were unblinking as she made her way through the maze of streets and back doubles that only weeks of well rehearsed navigation and ingrained familiarity can breed. The rain lashed the car as it made into fast turns and blind hairpin bends yet stealthily avoiding small obstructions and outcrops that Mercedes knew instinctively were there.

Within ten minutes the Vega was hurtling past the old manure hut in the mouth of the woods and up through Jade Intersection. A red light stood like an impotent century at the junction as the engine noise shifted a gear and sped through it, spraying a small bloodstained path and the remnants of an upturned burnt out car at the side of the road. The rain continued in a relentless barrage of defiance in this temporary midnight. It was as if the sun had been blotted out by volcanic ash. Great rivers of water with hellish torrent gushed down the sides of all the roads and available gullies as the Vega took another sharp bend. The back of it slew in the road, its weather beaten almost treadles tyres loosing purchase on the asphalt and mud that was quickly turning into a gritty paste. The Vega self corrected and on it went. Its rusted and creaking suspension coils dipped hard with an unexpected furrow in the road, coughing off flakes of brown detritus with a thud as Mercedes was thrown forward against the dashboard. Her chin struck the steering wheel and bruised on impact. She put her left hand out to grasp the freefall and it struck the central console twisting a finger into a painful crack that did not break it but activating the cheap RadioShack set. The noise of a screaming guitar chord filled the car that tapered off into a bounding base and snare drum of some melancholic trance track. The drum was beating in time with the frantic rhythm of the wipers. Vision was almost impossible as she leaned toward the windscreen to see further forward. Her shaking hand scrambled to find the radio control but it was jammed. She couldn't afford to look and check. The music thundered on. There was a sudden crashing noise as the Vega tore through a wooden fence ripping two metal wires that momentarily gripped the small radiator grill like cheese wires before turning blue and sparking free. The wires flayed and spat blue arcs as they kissed the passing wet metal and road and then they lay fighting like two Cobras in a fighting frenzy to the death. The car slew to a standstill outside the great auditorium. As Mercedes emerged from the car the screaming guitars and drums echoed across the complex in a competition with the lashing rain and running water that was everywhere. A shaft of yellow and red light broke through the volcanic ash clouds above as Mercedes removed from the boot another larger aluminium and rubberised flight case, her hair and make up hung with the sadness of a clown that had been just drenched by a bucket of water and flour by an unhappy audience. She ran to the auditorium, music still thumping from the little drowned Vega, its boot gaping open into the wet darkness like a thirsty insect.

She entered a labyrinth of corridors walking with purpose and determination, her head and neck held straight like a marching soldier. She turned from left to right, another right and two more lefts without hesitation or need to get her bearings. The soles of her military stealth boots squeaked and squelched against the floor. Her hair was wet and wild, her eyes as black as her heart as she pushed open a door leading to a private locker room. The droning beat from the car stereo still echoed through her mind despite it being now totally out of ear shot. Her heart was racing.

She pulled on the ninja silks over the ballistic weave canvass jumpsuit. Damp patches like phantoms appeared through the silk almost immediately as she pulled the silk white gloves on. Snapping open a small acrylic case she removed a blue cabochon ring. She briefly surveyed the inner inscription, 'Novus Ordo Seclorum", it read. She slipped it onto the third finger of her right hand and removed from the locker a fighting staff. She whipped it a few times through her nimble fingers, tossing it from left to right and left again. It span like a propeller blade through the air and ended up under her right arm pit in a horizontal position as she took up an imaginary fighting stance with an invisible opponent.

The double doors of the auditorium burst open as Mercedes parried her way into the middle of it. She was still wet and her boots made squeaking and straining noises as she danced a fantastic ballet of engagement with the air around her.

Longinner was sat in his locker room, his head in his hands when he heard the volley of noises from the great apexed hall. His resigned face lifted in disbelief. "What?" he muttered to himself. He tentatively picked himself up and walked slowly with his staff and a sense of unease to the great hall.

He pushed the double doors open as the stranger turned to face him from the centre of the hall. The figures fighting staff stopped motionless like the freeze frame of a film. There was no detectable movement at all, just a slow drop of water breaking from a knot of wet tangled hair that poked from beneath her head covering at the back. The orb of wetness smashed into the ground like a light bulb crashing into a graveyard of others. Maurice's face had fear in it. He had no face covering on to hide it from this stranger. He had not been expecting anyone; his guard was down and part of his ability to bluff and feign was missing. The figure moved a squelching boot and Maurice flinched. The micro movement had been intentional and designed to illicit a reaction from Maurice; the opponent. He could feel his heart beat high in his neck against the high silk collar like the trapped wings of a butterfly. He slowly and reluctantly stepped forward and brought the staff into a preparatory ready position. The figure suddenly moved with an unexpected ferociousness that had a certain nimble clarity that Maurice had not seen for a long long time. The last time had been from a very great master. He suddenly felt lost and the same as the first time he wore the ninja silk and had come before the great master who was to become his mentor, but he did not know this person, did not recognise the gait or stature. His fears were confirmed when he caught sight of the blue stoned tiger eye ring adorning the grip of the fighter. He stood some twenty feet away from the figure. He bowed. His eyes followed the stillness of the figure that did not return the customary pleasantry as he did so. He drew a semi-circle in mid air about eighteen inches above the ground with his staff and waited.

The two butterfly wings under his collar were beating now as if they were just about to have the life squeezed out of them, and they were at the start of the final throws of death.

"W-who are you?"

The figure did not move. Another light bulb of water smashed into the ground. That was the trigger, the starting pistol!!

54

Platinum Blonde Robot

The night Brunner had spent in the Apex Hotel; Sabian had spent in the dig out with Bianco, Roger and Camilla. It was a cold and bitter night and the wind howled like a Hyena through the makeshift hole that had earlier acted as a chimney. Sabian could not sleep. He had desperately wanted to get back into the Marimba factory, but had finally taken the advice of Roger and Camilla and stayed away. At least for the time being. The place would be a hot bed of security after the recently discovered breaches and it would not surprise Sabian if already there was an army of Ninja out in the woods turning it over with a fine tooth comb, or hanging and waiting, camouflaged in the terrain and just waiting for them to emerge. It was still twenty four hours before Charlotte Mercedes would drive the little Facel Vega onto the dust just fifty yards away in the driving rain.

Camilla and Roger were sleeping in foil space blankets about ten feet away from Sabian. Bianco was sleeping about three feet away from his feet. A candle flickered along the mud and ragged lime walls, its almost last dying embers casting a warm orange glow. It illuminated Bianco's facial features with dancing shadows. Sabian lay looking at her, his head propped up in the fist of his left hand. She stirred in her sleep and turned on her back, twisting the thin silver foil blanket that surrounded her. As she twisted the foil got trapped and took on the contours of her body. Sabian scanned its entire length. He felt slightly guilty at this; at his voyeuristic tendency to want to linger a little longer. The shape of her figure encased in silver reminded him of the female robot in the old black and white film, 'Metropolis'. Sabian as he thought this drifted off in his imagination thinking about that robot as it sat on a podium and great silent sparks danced above its head. He was staring into a space just below her breasts when he had a sudden strange sense of being watched. His eyes flicked to Bianco's face. Both of hers were wide and staring back at him. They locked for a brief moment and then she turned, sighing and staring into the empty space above her. Sabian felt embarrassed at his perverted longing.

"You're just like the men in the Aphrodite Mister Joseph Sabian. Did you have a wank as well? Or hadn't you got that far yet? You did consider it, didn't you?" She stared indignantly up at the wooden planked ceiling. There was a brief silence. "You're a beautiful young woman, is it wrong of me to look?" She turned to face him. "Do you want a piece of my ass Mister Sabian?" Sabian thought, 'It had crossed my mind', but found the word "Sorry!" coming from his lips. He glanced at Roger and Camilla. Neither had stirred, not obviously anyway! Bianco was now shooting Sabian a hard stare as the last wax of the candle burned out to a thin black vapour of smoke plunging the pit into darkness. "If I feel any creature on me in the night I will have to assume that it is you Joseph Sabian; you pervert!" Sabian just stared into the darkness.

55

Chimpanzee or Aardvark

The next morning, the same morning as Peter Brunner had ordered room service, Sabian, Cellini, Folkestone and Dufus headed back to the Marimba plant. With relative and surprising ease they found their way back to the production line module unhindered. Sabian made Bianco and Camilla remain as look outs as he and Roger entered the business part of the plant. Both wore their face coverings. The production line was business as usual and they glided by with not even a second glance. As they entered Gruger's office, Roger passed Sabian a small black memory stick that he placed straight into the back of the lone laptop computer. The screen lit abruptly with twenty to thirty vertical rows of flashing and rotating numbers with a single sign on rectangular box in the middle of the image. Every three to five seconds a large cross appeared in the box. When all seven crosses lay in a single horizontal line 'Password Correct' flashed like a beacon on the screen. Sabian glanced at Roger, the small lines at the corners of his eyes said he was smiling. Roger then removed the memory stick and typed in a twenty digit alpha numeric code. The computer accepted it. Sabian looked back at him, this time with surprise. "It's that simple?"

"Yes, that simple. I've been trying to get into this office for days. The fact that you've now got Gruger's swipe card has made everyone's life that much easier. But we can't hang around in here, your little plastic magic marker, I'm sure must be flagged and even now there's probably problems on the way. I do not even want to think what they may be!"

"Me and you both!" said Sabian. Roger then quickly inserted a pink memory stick and a programme immediately started to upload. "It will take about two minutes."

"That's going to be a long two minutes."

The programme is completing the data stream very subtly. It's rather like changing a single strand on a human DNA genome. One subtle change is all you need and hey presto, no man but a Chimpanzee or an Aardvark."

"Aardvark?"

"Yes, Aardvark. This Trojan Horse is so subtle it shouldn't be picked up in any of their usual data checks and quality controls, but it will sure as damn turn the marimba gel into virtually inert goo, and when they send the same data stream to the other eagerly waiting cells, well they might as well be programming this weeks lottery numbers into their hard drives." Without warning Roger took something from his pocket, a small canvas bag. Sabian watched him as if he was about to be treated with a conjuring trick. Roger emptied the content into his hand, a ruby pendant. "It's synthetic, contains a circuit that's controlled by lasers. Again like the rings it's a copy, the real one went missing but we think it's with one of their leaders." Sabian was speechless as Roger placed the ruby into a pod at the back of the computer. Two lasers passed through it. Sabian's eyes slowly widened as he realised who was wearing an exact copy of this pendant. "Joseph, I give you the Scarlet Infinity!"

One minute passed and it seemed like a hundred. Sabian was staring with increasing frequency between the door and the computer screen. Roger just stared at the flashing display of hieroglyphs and data streams. He appeared calm and unruffled. The ruby glowed red hot.

"How can you just stand there like a statue?"

"It's quite simple Joe. If I die with the bursting open of that door, with that single act it would have been still all worth it. Even if we are stopped now the corruption we have caused will take them months to put right. We would have saved many many lives; we will be unsung and unknown heroes of course."

"Yes, I'd prefer not to be all the same. Surely they must have a back up programme?"

"You'd think so wouldn't you, but no. Everything shouldn't be backed up until the final stage of the process, just before they send the hellish thing to the other cells. They're just as afraid of a back up copy being found and compromised and reverse engineered, which is virtually what we did with a Marimba Sphere. That's always been the trade off."

"You seem very well versed in all this?"

"It's taken up the last two years of my life, I would—- done!" The computer screen closed down and Roger whipped the key from the back port.

"Come on Joseph lets' go. The deed as they say is done thank you very much."

Camilla and Bianco had remained outside the door. No one came or left. When the door eventually opened it was Joe and Roger. The four fled from the complex. No alarm sounded and no pursuers pursued.

As they ran across the dust back to the woods Joseph Sabian slowed down. Roger turning said, "What you doing, can't hang around now!"

"I've a score to settle. You three go ahead. I'll meet you at the dig out when I've seen to Longinner."

"Don't worry about him, he's just a pawn in a very big game." said Camilla. Bianco had also now slowed her pace as she seemed undecided to stay with Sabian or the others. Sabian signalled without speaking with his eyes for her to remain with the other two.

"Good luck!" she whispered.

He ran back to the complex and tore a right toward the Great Auditorium. The others made their way back to the dig out where they remained for the rest of the day until they had to evacuate due to heavy rain. Sabian had made his way there as it was the only place he could feel relatively safe; the only place that would give him at least one appearance of Longinner if he was prepared to wait long enough. He waited in an unguarded stairwell. It was warm and dry and a far cry from the confines of the damp atmosphere of the dig out, that even now made his throat feel arid and hoarse. After about half an hour he had an irresistible urge to sleep. He initially fought against this but his eyelids felt heavier by the second and he felt comfortably woozy as his eyes flicked backwards and forwards like heavy metal ball bearings in their sockets. Soon he was experiencing micro sleeps; brief moments where consciousness was lost with almost no recollection and then with the drop of his head and the wet slap of his jaw against his chest he was gone. He remained in that position undisturbed.

Bianco was becoming impatient after several hours of waiting in the dig out. Her left leg bounced at an annoyingly frantic rate. The result of boredom, apprehension and anxiety is what Roger put it down to. Both Camilla and Roger had sat reading from the moment they had arrived back at the hole. The hours had slowly ticked by and Bianco had taken herself up and out into the woods on at least three occasions. Each occasion had been against the wishes of the other two. Each time she arrived back unharmed the others breathed an unnoticed sigh of relief. Then went back to reading their books. They then came a heavy down pour of rain that first came to notice with the sound of scurrying in the woods as various animals made their way fast back to their retreats and holes. The sound of the woods grew still and quiet in the second before the torrent hit it. At first the dark and dirty little hole in the ground was safe from the onslaught, saved by the umbrella of trees high above. This did not last. After about three to four minutes the water had broken the backs of the great leaves that had slowly at first, dipped like tongues in sick heads and then vomited their content on the ground below. A thousand or more tongues vomited in the same manner. The water gathered at first at the feet of the great trees in gullies that were hundreds of years old formed by the bony fingers of their roots. Soon the banks of the gullies were broken and small rivulets and trickles cut down the four lime and dirt walls of their hole that had been home. Roger was the first to notice. "We can't stay here tonight." He said gesturing with his forehead. The streams became thunderous and had now begun to fill up small pockets of disturbed earth on the floor of the dig out. Bianco still appeared nervous and impatient. She was also very tired of these games. She had not had the training that the others had had. Soon there were great platoons of running water racing down the four walls of the hole. There were so many and they were now so close that in some cases they had merged to form great sheets of rushing water.

"I think we're filling up. Time to leave!" said Camilla.

Bianco said: "Thank goodness!" as they all stood to form a queue for the makeshift ladder. Roger said: "We'll have to make our way to the Calista, I can't think of anywhere else that's going to be safe at the moment. Our hotel is certainly not going to be. I'm sure we would have all been rumbled by now"

"What's the Calista?" asked Bianco.

"It's a boat" replied Camilla.

"It's a motor boat" said Roger. "It's where Sabian and his team have been staying. It's our best chance of a dry night. But first we've got to get to Sabian. Once we find him, we're out of here and back home to the good old USA!."

As they emerged one by one from the hole in the ground there was a distant sound of a car engine and music thumping from overstretched speakers from near the Auditorium. Their ninja silks were no match for the rain and within seconds they were soaked through to the skin, the silk like wet tissue hugging their cold bodies.

Through a small clearing in the woods they saw a female emerge from a battered old sports car and remove from the boot hatch a silvered brief case. The rain pelted and music boomed in the din. None of the three recognised Charlotte Mercedes as she sprinted away from the sports car leaving its boot open to the driving rain. They would not have recognised her even if she was stood in front of them. None of then knew her or of her existence.

"Who is that?" said Camilla.

"Don't know!" replied Roger.

"I've not seen her at the Aphrodite, unless she's one of Longinner's new girls, but they certainly wouldn't be out here, that's for sure!" said Bianco.

Roger replied, "No time to speculate. I think we're going to have to get a little closer. Sabian could be in more trouble than we imagined."

The three ran to the tired looking drenched sports car with its open mouth. The music was tapering off to a hypnotic resonating slow drum beat. It stopped abruptly. There followed a welcoming silence. Bianco appeared deeply miserable.

"Can we get somewhere dry please, and quickly; what about the entrance Sabian took?" she said. The three found shelter in the same stairwell that Sabian had already vacated about an hour earlier.

"Where do you think he's got to?" said Bianco.

Roger said: "He's probably stalking Longinner, planning how he's going to assassinate him. He may have already have done the deed. More worrying is that he might be dead himself. I'm sure that's only a remote possibility though. If not an impossible one."

Camilla said: "Thanks for that!" and Bianco tried desperately to conceal a single tear that under the circumstances would have been mistaken for rainwater in any case. They remained huddled in the semi-darkness. Roger handed out the last of a set of foil blankets which they wrapped around themselves. They remained there for a further fifteen minutes.

56

What do you want from me?

Charlotte Mercedes was half smiling under her mask as she reigned down the first blow toward her opponent, Maurice Longinner. He blocked the force of it with his fighting staff and felt the ensuing onslaught vibrate through his wrist and body like a cannon going off in his torso. The minuet fleeting stillness of her move was that of a master and the shockwave turned his feet to lead and his heart missed a beat. When next the thud of the tight muscle in his chest came it beat within the pit of his stomach. The blue cabochon ring was only inches from his naked white face. Its surface vibrated lightly, and he saw the brown female eyes through the letterbox opening of his opponent's mask. A voice, stern and controlled came from under the opening. "Novus Ordo Seclorum; you bastard!" Longinner's face changed a lighter shade of pale and his heart misfired again. He wanted to speak but the words would just not come. How was this? What had he done to loose her affection? What about his money and his new life? There was then a rain storm of blows from every angle which he blocked with a great wall of metallic ringing. But he was on autopilot, his senses and passion had definitely been switched into neutral. A blow winded him in the gut and he grasped for his breath, dropping his staff. He fell to his knees clutching his throat and straining air into his lungs that just would not fill over the restricted muscles of his throat. "Why?" he strained out. Mercedes watched him with a look of utter contempt walking around him in circles. Still he could not breathe properly.

"The Organisation is not pleased with your conduct Maurice. I am not pleased with your conduct. It would seem that you have been overstepping your authority in many areas. Helping yourself to funds. Employing idiots. Did you know Flagg nearly raped and killed me? I've been working deep cover with the secret services of two countries, but I didn't really expect my end game to be in a room with a psychopath with a knife and a hard on, you are now in a room with a psychopath with a hard on Maurice. How does it feel? Please tell me!" His breathing was now regular but shallow. Mercedes picked his fighting staff from the floor and threw it like a javelin across the auditorium where it found purchase between two ornate carvings about fifteen feet from the ground on the west wall. "You won't be needing that anymore. Ever!" Maurice looked up at her as she moved slowly like a panther around him. He felt weak. His spirit had been broken. He was not used to this. He was the winner in everything he did. That only made him feel deeper in his own pit of despair. "What do you want from me?"

"I think the question would be more suitably phrased as what do I not want. It would be far quicker and simpler to answer that question. I do not want your dreams and your convictions. I want everything else, even your life. There will be no loose ends." Slowly he began to rise to his feet; both his legs were unsteady and shaking. Mercedes stopped her orbit around him and raised the tip of her staff so it touched the underside of his chin. She lifted his chin ever so slightly, teasing him with her authority over him. "Take what you want, I don't care!" "Oh, I intend to, I intend to!" She pulled her face covering off and stared into his eyes. Her hair was wet and wild. Longinner felt as if he was staring into the eyes of Medusa, with her fiery snakes moving around her head, each with its own bite and venom. They hissed at each other and then turned to face him spitting in rhythmic dances.

"Charlotte!" Sabian's voice echoed across the great hall. She turned to face him. The snakes stopped hissing but continued to dance in slower pulses. Mercedes eyes did not blink as she stared into the eyes of Joseph Sabian and through them. Longinner's face had sight hope in it, but only slight. Mercedes continued to talk, but she was still addressing Longinner but looking at Sabian. "Did you know who Gruger was Maurice?" Longinner did not answer. "He was my second, not you as you always mistakenly thought, and you killed him!" Sabian started to walk towards the two of them. "Ah, ah Joseph, stay exactly where you are." Sabian stopped, "Where is Peter, what have you done with him?"

"He is sleeping a long sleep Joseph, but of course you already knew that didn't you?"

"You murdering bitch!" Longinner saw an opportunity to get away and was just about to make the move when Mercedes started to spin. The end of her staff ejected a small three inch blade that locked into place a fraction of a second before it severed Longinner's jugular. "Weren't expecting that one were you Maurice? Goodnight." Longinner only had a second to register the thick spurt of blood and a metallic dullness before his vision was entombed in a heavy blackness that was to last for an eternity.

"You look surprised Mister Sabian."

"I could shoot you if I wanted from this distance."

"I dare say you could."

Sabian took out the small black handgun from inside his top. Its metal was warm from nestling in the holster under his arm for hours. He flicked a switch and Mercedes smiled the smile of an insane woman as a single red dot danced on her upper breasts and neck.

"Answer me one question, is Peter Brunner dead?"

"He is not dead Mister Sabian. How could I kill a man I am in love with? Our status and frames of reference have nothing to do with mutual and physical attraction. Isn't that a rule you've lived by most of your adult life Joseph?"

"I don't think we're particularly in the same league Charlotte? Is that your real name, Charlotte Mercedes?"

"You'll have to work that one out for yourself I'm afraid. I'm not giving you anymore clues to the whys and the wherefores." She started to walk toward him.

"Stay where you are." The safety switch clicked on his gun. This time the red dot danced in the middle of her forehead. She stopped and threw her staff to the ground in an act of defiance. "Shoot me then Joseph, but understand this, if you do that you will be dead to. Do you want to know why? I'm sure you do?" Sabian had a quizzical look on his face. "Shall I show you?" she continued. At that she ripped open her silk top to reveal the webbing underneath. "See these webbing pockets Joseph, each has about four Marimba Spheres in them. Now that's four pockets, I make that sixteen spheres don't you? Now what kind of an explosion do you think that would cause? Just one sphere would devastate this building. So before you think of filling me with lead, just remember you won't have much time, if any, after my dead weight hits the ground and fractures these fragile egg shells."

"You're bluffing, I don't see any spheres. That's just a webbing vest with pockets." Mercedes slowly reached into a top opening and removed a blue marble like sphere and gingerly placed it back where it made a clinking noise.

"Do you think I'm bluffing now Joseph?"

"You're fucking insane!"

"Perhaps, but just look at your own life Joseph and the life Peter Brunner lives. What thanks do you get? Who really cares anyway? You and your high moral ground. What double standards you have."

"Is the free lecture over?"

"Anytime you want it to be, just give me the nod or the spark from your metal."

Sabian seeing he was in a no win situation ran back through the door behind him as fast as his feet could carry him. Mercedes stood in the middle of the Great Auditorium laughing. It could have easily been mistaken for a sob. He ran out onto the dust of the complex. It was raining hard outside. He saw the Vega with its gaping boot and jumped into it hoping he could hot wire it. The battery was dead. He ran back to the woods and the dig out but it was just a swirling swamp of debris that the others had abandoned. 'Got to make sure Peter is okay', he thought as he went back out into the gloom and downpour of the cold Mauritian evening. He ran towards the bay where he was going to have to swim again to get back to the Calista. He did not envy the prospect in the slightest. The water was cold and as he swam he periodically used the lights from the Ingersoll watch to light his immediate surroundings.

Charlotte Mercedes stood in the dimly lit locker room and took out the inert spheres from her jacket and carefully placed them back into their egg box type compartments in the rubberised flight case. It was divided into three separate areas. One area contained the inert spheres that she had just returned. The larger area was empty and was space enough for small personal belongings and her ninja tools. The inside lid of the case had a dozen or so gleaming silver throwing stars all neatly tucked into fabric pockets that revealed the upper teeth in the frightening smiles of the wicked. The last compartment in the case was much smaller than the other two and could only be opened by entering a code. There was a digital temperature gauge on the locked stainless steel hatch. Mercedes fleetingly eyed the reading up after removing a layer of moisture condensation off the thin screen with her gloved thumb. She entered the code and clicked the hatch open. A fine gas mist came from inside. Nestled in cushioned compartments were three Marimba Spheres, with a loose plastic see through cover over them which read "Don't touch, danger of death" She turned quickly, disturbed by a noise from near the door. The door stood open to a six inch gap and a slight breeze filtered in from the corridor. Roger, Camilla and Bianco clung to each other in a small space behind four lockers on the other side of the room trying to work out what this woman was up to. Half entering the room by default more than design. Charlotte moved to the door and closed it with a firm slap. Bianco thought she was going to pass out the longer she held still with her breathing. If Mercedes had bothered to look a little further to her left she would have seen the three of them frozen like mannequin dummies in a shop window. But she did not look. She dismissed the door as a fluke to do with the strange weather and turned back to her case and spheres. She was just about to seal the case up when she thought she heard another noise coming from the depths of the corridor. She slowly put the lid of the case back down and opened the door of the locker room where she slowly tip toed its full ten yards to a dog leg and a further five feet to a door that was ajar and rhythmically catching on the metal of its frame ever so slightly. She opened it and peered out. The rain continued to lash, and when the door was open a gust of wind caught it like a sail opened to full mast. Mercedes was pulled out onto the dust which was now like bonded cement. She hit the ground with a thud. The others had quickly moved from their hiding place in the instant Mercedes was out of sight and well into the corridor. They made a cursory look around. Roger had found another door and summoned the other two over. Camilla was holding the blue stoned ring that Charlotte had left and was speculatively comparing it to the replica that she had been issued. The differences when placed side by side were enormous. The shanks on the fake were less steep and the stone very fractionally smaller. Perhaps they'd been rumbled much further back than any of them could guess. Bianco was looking at the compartments in the case and the one with the fine mist coming out she had open to a crack when Camilla said "For god sake, don't touch that; let's just get out of here!"

57

Checking on Peter

Sabian was cramping in his carves as he swam on. He tried to ignore the tugging at the muscles, but had to stop. He knew all too well what a full constriction of the muscle felt like. It rendered you useless and in so much pain. He stopped for a couple of minutes, treading water with his arms only and trying as best he could to massage each muscle in turn; an almost impossible feat. He then swam on. He activated the lights of the watch again as he saw the Calista in the distance. He was now down to a painful doggy paddle and breast stroke without using his legs. The lights of the watch had grown dim and would soon be virtually useless without a charge. Just one more stroke he kept telling himself. Nearly there, nearly there. His head struck the white body of the hull. He looked up at it and it could have been a great ocean going vessel like the QE2 or something similar, with its peaked bow. It also looked like a very large sharks' tooth from his perspective. He did not have the strength to pull himself up by the rope ladder.

"Peter, Peter." He shouted. There was no answer. He repeated the chant but still nothing came. "Damn it, going to have to climb the ladder!" he muttered under his breath. His legs were almost cramping again and he had to pull himself up the side of the rope ladder as if it were a single rope but using the struts every now and again to relieve the pressure from his aching arms. He pulled himself onto the deck. "Peter are you okay, please answer me?" Still no reply. He lay on his back for a good five minutes to get his breath and get some strength back into his limbs.

Mercedes pulled herself up from the wet mud that now clung to her hair face and clothing. She was not pleased with the situation. She secured the door behind her and made her way back along the corridor to the locker room. She went to click the ring back into its acrylic holder but as she went to pick it up she studied it briefly. 'Surely I left it near the case not on this table'. She mused on the point a moment before slipping it into the small container and snapping its lid shut. She placed it into the flight case, secured the Marimba compartment and closed the lid, spinning its combination tumblers to random settings. She entered the great hall for one last time carrying the case. Longinner's body was sprawled like a rag doll with a pool of dirt red blood surrounding him from all approaches. She grimaced as she leant over him and lifting his hand she pulled off the large stoned ring and placed it into a webbing pocket of her jacket. She did not regard the traitor anymore, and turning her back on him she walked away like a military general on a mission.

Sabian almost fell down the stairs leading to the Calistas' main cabin. Peter was out cold. Sabian felt for a pulse. There was one but it was extremely thready and weak. "Peter, Peter wake up, wake up will you!" Still he did not stir. Sabian noticed the puncture mark and bruising on his left forearm. "Jesus Christ, what has she done?"

He dragged Peter to the shower unit and turned on the ice cold water onto his head and shoulders. After a minute or so he started to come around, by spitting bubbles of water.

"What! What's going on?"

"Peter, Peter, you need to wake up. Wake up now will you! Do not sleep!"

Peter was groggy and his eyes lids flickered like heavy wooden shutters in the wind, slamming up and down in irregular bouts. "Am I dreaming again?"

"No you're not dreaming. We need to get out of here. You've been injected with something and I need to get you some medical attention."

"Injected, injected by who?"

"Charlotte Mercedes, that's who. She's working for the dark side my friend. I would forget her if I were you."

"This is a dream, isn't it? Charlotte wouldn't hurt me. What are you talking about?"

"I can't go into it all at the moment. We just have to leave". At that Sabian started to try and lift Peter. "No no, what the hell is going on? What's Charlotte done? What has she been up to Sabian?"

"As I said, she's working for the other side. She's their top woman. I'd forget her if I were you. She's just killed Longinner who was working for her."

"Killed Longinner, what are you talking about? You need to slow down mate, please!"

"We haven't got time for this shit Peter. We need to move and move now. They'll be plenty of time for small talk later." Peter grunted at that with a bemused look on his face and rose to his feet shaking with Sabians' assistance. "Where are we going?" Peter said in a flat tone. "Not really sure, The Palm maybe? It still won't be that safe, but anywhere is better than here. I doubt we'll get booked in anywhere this time of week."

"We might, I remember I saw a sign a couple of days ago saying there were beach huts for hire just on the other side of the bay. Bit of a walk though from here. Not sure I'll be able to make it Joe."

"You will, believe me!"

After about forty minutes of walking with Sabian half carrying Peter at times they found themselves at a small beach cove area where they waited patiently for a further twenty minutes as per a timetable on a nearby post advertising the huts. Much to Peter's delight a man arrived and after a brief conversation and an exchange of money they were shown down the steps into the cove to the vacant beach hut that stood on wooden stilts and was decked with a veranda. It was the sort of place that one would find in the Maldives on an expensive yet basic package holiday. After the man had shown the two of them to the door he left without as much as a goodbye. Sabian lowered Peter onto the bed who was exhausted with pain and groggy still.

"What is really going on Sabian?"

"I'm going to have to leave you here for awhile and find the others and bring them back here. Our job is done here and we need to get home."

"What others? Who are you talking about?"

"I found, well they found me actually, our friends from the CIA that I told you about. They weren't dead after all. They've got a woman with them as well. We all need to get off this island and on a big white bird home. I need to get you some medical attention as well."

"And Charlotte is she fixed in with this little plan of yours?"

"No, obviously not. Don't be fooled by her Peter. She's as good as dead now!"

58

Earning the Queen's Shilling

Several days later and on the same morning that Holly Troupe was studying the stranger in the Portico Café who was wildly drawing imaginary symbols in the air bad things were happening elsewhere. Rome, Paris, Los Angeles, Sydney, Johannesburg and London were all seats of impending change and disaster. Shortly before nine ten hours on that morning three remote control ten to one scale Hummer vehicles filtered down a ramp from a goods vehicle parked in a side street off Leicester Square. It was about six hours GMT. These small toys were about twelve inches long and each filled with a deadly cargo. Six Marimba Spheres nestled together in each vehicles body. Packed with bubble wrap and wadding to prevent early detonation. The three vehicles scrambled over the cobbled pavement of a side street in single file. Each was fitted with a forward looking CCTV camera. The motors screamed like the high pitch of chainsaws as each Hummers six black rubber wheels bounced and bounced on the uneven surfaces below. Soon the three entered the Square itself to the bemusement of onlookers as the three separated on different journeys. Some people laughed and pointed, others looked around for the person who was controlling them. Some dodged out the way. The feeling mainly was one of irritation and annoyance as people filtered off to their soulless existences. One man was so annoyed he kicked the passing black Hummer because it had impeded his passage. One of the Spheres in side lightly clinked against another through an opening in the wadding. Each orb was now a swirling typhoon as the gel in them mixed with the fury of the vehicles motion and poor suspension. An off duty police sergeant on her way to a briefing at New Scotland Yard paused and looked at the motion of the commuters moving out of the way of something she could not quite see. She pulled herself into the recess of a shop doorway to prevent herself from being knocked and jostled by the continuous stream of anonymous humanity. She could now hear the light buzz of something and looked from left to right and up and down, but could still not work out what the source was. There was another laugh from an opening in the crowd about thirty feet away with people now stopping and talking in small huddles. The whine of the thing was getting closer. Then she saw it, not quite able to make anything of it. With a sudden bounce the remote control toy struck the wall of the Capital Radio studio building and rebounded back about six inches, each wheel in a rhythmic pulse of self correction. She too looked around trying to identify in the crowds and huddles a potential controller. No aerial was visible or other clue above the sea of miserable faces. The Hummer then moved very slowly toward the wall, the whine of its motor seemed to step up several gears as a huge fan in the middle of its body activated and started to suck the air from underneath it like a vacuum cleaners efficient suction system. The front wheels of the Hummer started to climb the side of the building until it was at a precarious forty five degrees with the angle of the wall and pavement. Again the gears stepped up and the fan span furiously. People were now stood transfixed looking at the thing as it hugged the wall and started to move up the sheer vertical incline very slowly. The spheres rattled around inside clinking against each other and the hard plastic metal cavities inside, as bubble wrap and wadding had separated from their prizes. A uniform constable on the other side of the Square had been drawn by the crowd. Trying to work out what all the interest was. Was it someone collapsed or a disturbance perhaps? The off duty sergeant had moved out of the recess and was now trying to create distance between herself and the Hummer with her mobile phone tightly held in her fist.

Commissioner Charles Blake was just sitting down to a light breakfast of black coffee and toast in his office at the Yard when the phone rang with the information that Charing Cross's Duty Inspector had just made a decision to evacuate Leicester Square and the streets surrounding.

A snake of blue lights tore up the Mall, through Whitehall towards Trafalgar Square. The snake broke in two. One took St Martins in the Field, the other entered Leicester Square. Officers from Commissioners' Reserve entered on foot with loud hailers clearing the masses. Cordons were put up to prevent others entering the area. People were held back by flickering blue tape, argumentative and seething at the break in their timetables. A scuffle broke out in Birdcage Walk as a young PC tried to explain to a baying crowd the importance of staying behind his tape. A man in an expensive business suit and silver Samsonite briefcase lifted the tape to remonstrate with the constable. His job was far too important for all this shenanigans. He pushed the officer in the chest who fell to the ground. Another officer ran over and detained the man who had to be restrained to apply handcuffs. "Is this what I pay my taxes for?" screamed Mr Samsonite.

The black Hummer now clung like a limpet some fifty feet above the ground to the side of the Capital Radio building. It and the surrounding buildings had been evacuated. The Square was a ghost town. The other two Hummers had climbed two other buildings across the Square to form a triangle of devastation. Their fans and motors screamed in the empty solitude. A small explosives robot shuttled across the Square in fits and starts toward the studio wall. Once it was parallel with the wall and directly under the Hummer a small head with mounted remote CCTV turned skyward toward the black insect some sixty feet above it. The explosives officer viewed the image on a monitor several streets away cocking his head from side to side looking for clues, anything that would provide an in road. He turned to the Duty Inspector. "We could wait a bit longer if you like, or I could blow the thing now?" He said. The Inspector looked at the explosives officer pensive and not saying a word. "It's your call!" said the explosives officer, "I've given you the options." Inspector Garrett glanced at his watch. It was nine twenty seven. Garrett glanced at Sergeant Wicks. "We're certainly earning the Queen's shilling today John!" he said.

At 930 all four devices exploded. The Hummers fell from their towers crashing to the ground. The spheres inside of them hissing and spitting but not fully functional. They crashed like cartons of fresh eggs, impotent and worthless, spilling their goods onto pavements. Similar scenes raged across the globe.

Sabian finished sending his transmission from the Palm as Brunner burst into the room. His limp was still prominent. "Sabian there's been an explosion, and I've been hearing rumours that it's been happening every-where."

"I think we've done an incredibly commendable job Peter. The Spheres have been worthless, or at least drastically reduced in their power. Camilla and Roger have gone home and are safe. My only regret is Bianco was killed today."

"I'm sorry to hear that Joe, I know you had a soft spot for her. I wish I could have met her. How did it happen?"

"She brought a sphere to the beach hut. She didn't really know what the thing was. None of us had taken the time to tell her. She was only trying to be helpful. Probably picked the thing up the time we were in the Marimba plant. It was an earlier generation sphere, not one of the dampened down versions that we influenced."

"I'm really really sorry, she had family didn't she?"

"Yes a grandmother in Switzerland. I've sent a message via Interpol but I've decided to fly out there myself and deliver the news."

"That's very noble of you Joseph. She really shouldn't have been mixed up in all this business in the first place."

"We're you followed Peter do you know?"

"Why do you ask?"

"It was just something someone said to me a short while ago. A little problem I had to sort out."

"I wasn't aware of being followed."

"Good, that's excellent! Time for a drink don't you think?"

"Shouldn't we stay here in hiding for awhile?"

"I think we've done enough of that Peter already. We both need to relax a bit, get a good night sleep and get the hell out of here, wouldn't you agree?"

"Joe I can't stop myself from thinking about Charlotte and everything you've told me about her. I wish you were all wrong on that score. I am in love with her. I can not stop myself. It is eating me up inside."

"You're a good man Peter. You will find someone else."

"Will I? This last week has been the craziest one of my whole life. In a strange perverse way it has been enjoyable, an adventure."

"You've got the bug I'm afraid. I'm only really truly happy exploring the outer limits of danger. I remember when I was nineteen and I'd gone on an expedition of sorts with some friends in the Cheviot Hills. Myself and a friend got separated from the others. It was freezing; we were lost with only a few provisions. I remember clinging to the side of a mountain for dear life. My fingers had no feeling in them. All I craved for was to be back home at my parents and soak into a hot path and drift off with soft music playing. The irony of the whole thing was that when we eventually did make it back to safety and sanity I found myself in that bath some weeks later and all I wanted to do was cling to the side of that mountain and feel the uncertainty and danger before me. I've been the same ever since."

"I think I see where you're coming from."

"Do you? Do you really? There is one job that still isn't finished here. We could deal with it. It's unlikely another team will be despatched in time to strike while the iron is hot."

"What's that?"

"Charlotte Mercedes! The bitch needs to be killed!"

59

On a Wing and a Prayer

The next morning Joseph Sabian and Peter Brunner entered the airport terminus each carrying a small sports bag. Peter still had a slight limp. He looked miserable and bewildered. Sabian did not have any expression that would give his inner emotions away. They both made their way to the exclusive lounge on the third floor and sat drinking coffee staring out across the tarmac of the runways. The sun beat down and the drinking lounge was bright and had an orange glow. The two men did not speak. Much had been said and done in the previous week. Silence felt like a best friend. The room was air conditioned and comfortable. Peter felt like he could stay there a day or so just to gather his thoughts and try to anchor himself back into a reality that he knew and understood before he got on the plane back home. The coolness reminded him of the cab ride he had taken only a week earlier. How much had happened in that time. He could not work out if he was the same man or not. Only familiar surroundings would confirm or deny that particular aspect of who he was and who he was not. His flat back in Greenwich might as well have been on a different planet belonging to a different being, one he didn't recognise anymore. Perhaps he was being oversensitive or paranoid. Surely after a day or two of being back there that slow reality of Peter Brunner, the old Peter would return. But there was almost fear in that too. Did he really want what he had been? Did he want to become more of what he was becoming? If only it had had more time to mature he would know. So the reality was he reckoned to himself was that he was standing on a crossroads with two signs, one pointing back at his old life, the other to a dangerous and unknown territory. He was like a man standing on the beach looking out into the cold surf of the sea out to a small island. He could stare and stare. He could turn back and walk back up the beach. Or he could wade into the cold uninviting water up to his waist where small waves would crash against the small of his back with an unnerving coolness until he made a decision to drop and submerge himself into a temporary pain. The first few strokes would be the hardest. Coldness racking every sinew and muscle. But then when the blood started pumping the body would warm and soon he would be invigorated with a rush of life through him. He would pull himself up onto the new land and look back and feel victorious, knowing it was the journey that had made him, not his destination.

"Penny for your thoughts?" Sabian broke the silence. Peter did not answer. He stared at the Boeing 747 that soundlessly drifted in on a distant runway and another bus bringing in a new wave of tourists into the blistering heat. "I don't know what to do Sabian?"

"About her?"

"She's part of it, but I think it runs much deeper than that!"

"You need to let her go. There's a Charlotte Mercedes in every country I've been to, in every failed and successful mission. You're a hero now Peter. We have saved so many lives. Ultimately that's more important isn't it?"

"Is it, I'm not really sure?"

"Another coffee?"

"Yeah, okay." Sabian picked himself up rubbing his hands hesitantly down his upper legs not sure whether to leave his friend or not. He then walked reticently over to the bar drawing his wallet from his back pocket. Peter took from his pocket a small silver chain. It had two pendants, one a small oval Saint Michael, a present he'd been given on his promotion. The other was a silver bullet with Flagg's name engraved into the side. It was the only thing he had left of Charlotte. He ran his finger and thumb over the raised image of Saint Michael with his staff slaying the dragon below his horse. Saint Michael, the patron saint of police officers. He then ran his fingers along the bullet and the rough cut inscription of the name that he hated so much. He could feel the raised metal of the letters and thought if he pushed hard enough the metal would cut his fingers. There was a second when he felt tempted. Peter was not a religious man. There it was again that juxta position. That crossroads with its two signs. How two simple objects could hold so much symbolism in a single moment made his stomach feel like it was filled with hot lead. Sabian returned and handed Peter a blue Mauritian airlines cardboard cup that was steaming and rested a reassuring hand on his left shoulder. Peter took a sip of coffee and slipped the chain back into his pocket.

The stewardess went through the safety procedure. She had eye contact with Sabian and Peter thought he was now flirting with her from his seat. Peter was not listening to anything. The runway fell away as the plane raised itself into the cloud covering. After a few minutes it levelled off and the engine noise changed as the safety belt lights went off and the small little island mass changed to an impotent blob and then a speck and then vanished over the horizon. Peter excused himself from Sabian who was now staring deeply into the eyes of the Stewardess who was serving him vodka and tonic water. The name Barbara shimmered on the badge of her left breast. Sabian tried to read it from four inches away, looked up and smiled. He did not notice Peter leaving. Peter locked himself in the toilet cubicle and stared at his face in the water flecked mirror. Standing he took the fragile chain and its cargo from his pocket and before leaving he paused, looked at the pendulums and dropped the thing into the bin under the sink. The chain fell amongst the used tissues. He then went back to his seat.

Three weeks passed and Peter drifted into his previous life. Days at the Yard. Late drinks in The Golden Hinde just near the Naval Museum in Greenwich. One night he returned home and was just about to place his key in the lock when he saw it. From the handle was the silver chain with its oval Saint Michael and silver bullet. It swayed gently. As he bent to touch the thing to see if it was real Charlottes' voice came from behind.

"Hello Peter" She said, lightly touching his shoulder.
"It is done my darling" she whispered.

FIN

"Scarlet Infinity" was started on 15th May 2007 and finished on 16th December 2007.

Joseph Sabian and Peter Brunner will return in:-

"The Face Man"

If you would like to be kept up to date about the release date of the 'The Face Man' then please send an email to: ScarletInfinity@googlemail.com

Printed in the United Kingdom by
Lightning Source UK Ltd., Milton Keynes
139743UK00001B/5/P